Journey to the Center of the Earth

by JULES VERNE

Abridged and Edited by Nora Kramer

SCHOLASTIC INC
New York Toronto London Auckland Sydney Tokyo

ISBN 0-590-04450-8

20 19 18 17 16 15 14 13 12 11   6 7 8/8

Printed in the U.S.A.   01

Contents

My Uncle Makes
a Great Discovery

Looking back to all that has occurred to me since that eventful day, it is hard to believe in the reality of my adventures. They were truly so wonderful that even now I am bewildered when I think of them.

My uncle, a German, had married my mother's sister, an Englishwoman. He was very much attached to me, and as I was an orphan as well as his nephew, he invited me to study under him in his home in Hamburg, Germany. He was a professor there of philosophy, chemistry, geology, mineralogy, and many other ologies.

One day, after spending some hours in the laboratory, I felt hungry and was about to go look for Martha, our old French cook and housekeeper, when my uncle, Professor Von Hardwigg, suddenly opened the street door, and came rushing upstairs.

"Harry — Harry — Harry — " he shouted.

I hurried to him, but before I could reach his room, he was stamping his foot on the landing.

"Harry!" he cried frantically, "are you coming up?"

At that moment I was far more interested in our dinner than in science, but my uncle was not a man to be kept waiting.

He was a very learned man and a most kind relative. I was bound to him by the double ties of affection and interest. I took deep interest in all his doings, and rarely was I absent from his lectures. Like him, I preferred geology and mineralogy to all the other sciences. I was anxious to gain *real knowledge of the earth.*

He corresponded with all the great, learned, scientific men of the age. I was therefore in constant communication, through their letters, with Sir Humphrey Davy, Captain Franklin, and other great men.

My uncle was fifty years old; tall, thin, and wiry. Large spectacles hid, to a certain extent, his huge restless eyes; his nose resembled a long thin file.

He lived in a very nice house, in that very nice street, the Konigstrasse, in Hamburg. Though lying in the center of town, it was perfectly rural in its aspect — half wood, half bricks, with old-fashioned gables — one of the few old houses spared by the great fire of 1842. It was a handsome house, though tottering and not exactly comfortable.

My uncle was rich, with a considerable private income. But to my notion, the best part of his possessions was his goddaughter, Gretchen. This young lady, the old cook, the professor, and I were the sole inhabitants of the big old house. With a little less of my uncle's fury, we should have been a happy family.

My uncle received me in his study, which was practically a museum. Though he had summoned me, he was already absorbed in a book.

"Wonderful!" he cried, tapping his forehead. "Wonderful — wonderful!"

The book was a yellow-leaved volume, and my uncle was in raptures over it. He repeated aloud, half a dozen times, that it was very, very old.

I asked him what it was.

"It is the *Heims-Kringla* of Snorre Tarleson," he said, "the celebrated Icelandic author of the twelfth century — it is a true and correct account of the Norwegian princes who reigned in Iceland."

He was delighted to have found the original work in the Icelandic tongue, which he declared to be one of the most magnificent and yet simple languages in the world.

"The letters," I said, "are rather difficult to understand."

"It is a Runic manuscript, the language of the original population of Iceland," cried my uncle, angry at my ignorance.

I was about to venture a joke when a small scrap of parchment fell out of the book. The professor seized it. It was about five inches by three, and was scrawled over in the most extraordinary fashion.

The lines on page 10 of this book are an exact facsimile of what was written on the piece of parchment — and they were to induce my uncle to undertake the most wonderful series of adventures which ever fell to the lot of human beings.

My uncle looked keenly at the document for some moments and then declared that it, too, was Runic. He pointed out that the letters were similar to those in the book, but then what did they mean? This was exactly what I wanted to know.

I was delighted to find that my uncle knew as much about the matter as I did — nothing.

"And yet," he muttered to himself, "it is old Icelandic. I am sure of it."

And my uncle ought to have known, for he was a perfect polyglot dictionary in himself. He did not pretend to speak the two thousand languages and four thousand dialects in the different parts of the globe, but he did know all the more important ones.

The clock struck two, and Martha, our old French cook, called out to let us know that dinner was on the table.

"Bother the dinner!" cried my uncle.

But I was hungry; I sallied forth to the dining room. Out of politeness I waited three minutes, but there was no sign of my uncle. I was surprised. For the sake of poring over this musty old piece of parchment, my uncle forbore to share our meal! To satisfy my conscience, I ate for both of us.

As I consumed the last apple and drank the last glass of wine, a terrible voice was heard. It was my uncle roaring for me to come to him. I made it in one leap, so loud, so fierce was his tone.

The Mysterious Parchment

"I declare," cried my uncle, striking the table fiercely with his fist, "I declare to you it is Runic — and contains some wonderful secret, which I must get at, at any price."

"Sit down," he said fiercely, "and write to my dictation."

I obeyed.

"I will substitute," he said, "a letter of our alphabet for that of the Runic. We will then see what that will produce. Now, begin and make no mistakes."

The dictation commenced with the following incomprehensible results:

mm.rnlls	nicdrke	.nscrc
sgtssmf	Saodrrn	eeutul
kt,samn	emtnael	oseibo
esruel	Atvaar	rrilSa
unteief	ccdrmi	ieaabs
atrateS	dt,iac	frantu
seecJde	nuaect	Kediil

My uncle snatched the paper from my hands and examined it with the most rapt and deep attention.

"I declare it puts me in mind of a cryptograph," he cried. "Unless the letters have been written without any real meaning; and yet, why take so much trouble? Who knows but I may be on the verge of some great discovery?"

My candid opinion was that it was all rubbish! But this opinion I kept carefully to myself.

"The cryptograph, if that is what it is, is of much later date than the book," he said. "It appears probable to me that this was written by some owner of the book. Now who was the owner, is the next important question. Perhaps by great good luck it may be written somewhere in the volume."

With these words, my uncle took off his

spectacles and examined the book carefully with a powerful magnifying glass.

On the flyleaf was a line of writing almost effaced by time. This was what he sought; and, after some considerable time, he made out these letters:

"Arne Saknussemm!" he cried in a joyous and triumphant tone. "That is not only an Icelandic name, but the name of a learned professor of the sixteenth century — a celebrated alchemist."

I bowed, a token of respect.

"This Saknussemm, nephew mine, may have hidden on this bit of parchment some astounding invention. I believe the cryptograph to have a profound meaning — which I must make out."

My uncle walked about the room in a state of excitement impossible to describe.

"It may be so, sir," I timidly observed, "but why conceal it?"

"Why — how should I know? Did not Galileo make a secret of his discoveries in connection with Saturn? But we shall see. Until

I discover the meaning of this sentence I will neither eat nor sleep."

"My dear uncle — " I began.

"Nor you either," he said.

It was lucky I had eaten for both of us that day.

"In the first place," he continued, "there must be a clue. If we could find that, the rest would be easy enough."

The prospect of going without food and sleep was not promising, so I determined to do my best to try to solve the mystery.

"This man Saknussemm," my uncle went on, "was a very learned man. He probably, like most learned men of the sixteenth century, wrote in Latin. If I am wrong in this, then we must try Spanish, French, Italian, Greek, and Hebrew. My own opinion, though, is decidedly in favor of Latin."

"Very probably," I replied, not to contradict him.

"Let us look into the matter," continued my uncle. "Here we have a series of one hundred and thirty-two letters, apparently thrown pell-mell upon paper — i.e., without organization. There are words which are composed wholly of consonants, such as *mm.rnlls*, and others which are nearly all vowels. Probably we shall find that the phrase is arranged according to some mathematical plan. No doubt a certain sentence has been written out and then jumbled up. Now, Harry, show your English wit — what is that plan?"

I could give him no hint. While he was speaking I had caught sight of the portrait of my cousin Gretchen, and was wondering when she would return. We were engaged, and loved one another very sincerely. But my uncle knew nothing of this.

Without noticing my abstraction, my uncle began reading the puzzling cryptograph in all sorts of ways, according to some theory of his own. Presently, rousing my wandering attention, he dictated one attempt to me.

I handed it over to him. It read as follows:

mmessunkaSenrA.icefdoK.segnittamurtn
ecertserrette,rotaivsadua,ednecsedsadne
lacartniiiluJsiratracSarbmutabiledmek
meretarcsilucoYsleffenSnl.

I could scarcely keep from laughing, but it put my uncle in a towering rage. He struck the table with his fist, darted out of the room, and out of the house. Taking to his heels he was presently lost to sight.

An Astounding Discovery

"What is the matter?" cried the cook, entering the room. "When will master have his dinner?"

"Never."

"And his supper?"

"I don't know. My uncle has determined to fast and make me fast until he makes out this abominable inscription."

"You will be starved to death," she said.

I sent her away, and began some of my usual work of classification. I thought of going out, but my uncle would have been angry at my absence. At the end of an hour, my allotted task was done. Lighting my pipe, and seating myself in the great armchair, I began to think.

I could easily imagine my uncle tearing along some solitary road, talking to himself, cutting the air with his cane, and still thinking of the absurd bit of hieroglyphics. Would he hit upon some clue, and come home in a better humor? Mechanically, I took up the puzzle and tried every imaginable way of grouping the letters. I put them together by twos, threes, fours, and fives. Nothing intelligible came out, except that the fourteenth, fifteenth, and sixteenth letters made *ice* in English; the eighty-fourth, eighty-fifth, and eighty-sixth, the word *sir*. Then at last I seemed to find the Latin words *rota, mutabile, ira, nec, atra.*

"Ha! there seems to be some truth in my uncle's notion," I thought as again I found the Latin word *luco,* which means sacred wood.

Then in the third line I made out *tabiled,* a perfect Hebrew word, and at the last, *mère arc, mer,* which were French.

It was enough to drive one mad. Four different languages in this absurd phrase. What connection could there be between ice, sir, anger, cruel, sacred wood, changing, mother, arc, and sea? The first and the last might, in a sentence connected with Iceland, mean sea of ice. But what of the rest of this monstrous cryptograph?

My brain was almost on fire. My eyes were strained from staring at the parchment.

The whole absurd collection of letters appeared to dance before my vision. I was stifling. I wanted air. I fanned myself with the document, seeing now the back and then the front.

Imagine my surprise when glancing back at the wearisome puzzle, the ink having gone through, I clearly made out the Latin words *craterem* and *terrestre*.

I had discovered the secret!

It came upon me like a flash of lightning. I had got the clue. All you had to do to understand the document was to read it backwards.

My delight, my emotion, may be imagined. My eyes were dazzled, and I trembled so that at first I could make nothing of it. One look, however, would tell me all I wished to know.

"Let me read," I said to myself, after drawing a long breath.

I spread the paper before me on the table. I passed my finger over each letter. In my excitement I read it out.

What horror took possession of my soul. I was like a man who had received a knockdown blow. Was it possible that I really read the terrible secret? Had it really been accomplished? A man had dared to do — what?

No living being should ever know.

"Never!" cried I, jumping up. "Never shall my uncle be made aware of the dread secret. He would be quite capable of undertaking the terrible journey. Worse, he would compel me to accompany him, and we should be lost forever. No! Such folly and madness cannot be allowed."

I was almost beside myself with rage and fury.

"My uncle is already nearly mad," I cried aloud. "This would finish him."

I snatched up book and parchment, and was about to cast them into the fire when the door opened and my uncle entered.

I had scarcely time to put down the wretched documents before he was by my side. His thoughts were bent on the terrible parchment. Some new combination had probably struck him while taking his walk.

Seating himself in his armchair, he began an algebraic calculation. I watched him with anxious eyes. My flesh crawled as it became probable that he would discover the secret.

For three hours he continued — without speaking a word or without raising his head — scratching, rewriting, calculating over and over again. I knew that in time he must hit upon the solution.

Time went on, night came, the sounds in the streets ceased. Still my uncle went on, not even answering our cook when she came to call us to supper.

I did not dare to leave him, so I waved her away, and at last fell asleep on the sofa.

When I awoke my uncle was still at work. His red eyes, his matted hair, his flushed cheeks showed how terrible his struggle had been during that long sleepless night. Though he was severe with me, I loved him and my heart ached at his suffering. I knew that by speaking one little word all this suffering would cease. But I could not speak it.

"Nothing shall make me speak," I muttered. "He will want to follow in the footsteps of the other! I know him well. His imagination is a perfect volcano, and to make discoveries in the interests of geology he would sacrifice his life. To reveal the secret would be suicidal. He would not only rush to destruction himself but drag me with him."

I crossed my arms, looked the other way, and smoked, resolved never to speak.

When our cook wanted to go out to market, she found the front door locked and the key taken away. Was this done purposely or not? Surely Professor Hardwigg did not intend the old woman and myself to become martyrs to his obstinate will. Were we to be starved to death?

I wanted my breakfast, and I saw no way of getting it. Still, I would starve rather than yield. The cook took me seriously to task. What was to be done? She could not go out, and I dared not.

My uncle continued counting and writing. He neither thought of eating nor drinking. In this way twelve o'clock came round. I was hungry. This could not go on. It did, however, until two, when my sensations of hunger were terrible. I began to think the document absurd. Perhaps it might be only a gigantic hoax. Very likely my uncle would make the discovery himself, then I should have suffered starvation for nothing. Under the influence of hunger this reasoning appeared admirable. I determined to tell all.

The question now arose as to how it was to be done. I was still dwelling on the thought when my uncle got up and put on his hat.

What! Go out and lock us in? Never!

"Uncle," I began.

He did not appear to hear me.

"Professor Hardwigg," I cried.

"What?" he retorted. "Did you speak?"

"How about the key?"

"The key of the door?"

"No, of these horrible hieroglyphics."

He looked at me from under his spectacles, then rushing forward he clutched me by the arm. His very look was an interrogation.

I simply nodded.

With an incredulous shrug of the shoulders, he turned on his heel. Undoubtedly he thought I had gone mad.

"I have made a very important discovery," I said.

His eyes flashed. His hand was lifted in a menacing attitude. For a moment neither of us spoke. It is hard to say which of us was more excited.

"You don't mean to say that you have any idea of the meaning of the scrawl?"

"I do," was my desperate reply. "Look at the sentence as dictated by you."

"But it means nothing," was the angry answer.

"Nothing if you read from left to right, but — "

"Backwards!" cried my uncle, in wild amazement. "O most cunning Saknussemm! I am such a blockhead!"

He snatched up the document, gazed at

it with haggard eyes, and read it out as I had done.

It read as follows:

In Sneffels Yokulis craterem kem delibat umbra Scartaris Julii intra calendas descende, audas viator, at terrestre centrum attinges. Kod feci.

Arne Saknussemm

Which dog-Latin, being translated, reads as follows:

Descend into the crater of Yokul of Sneffels, which the shade of Scartaris caresses before the kalends of July, audacious traveler, and you will reach the center of the earth. I did it.

Arne Saknussemm

My uncle leaped three feet from the ground. He rushed about the room, wild with delight and satisfaction. He knocked over tables and chairs. He threw his books about until at last, utterly exhausted, he fell into his armchair.

"What's the time?" he asked.

"About three."

"My dinner does not seem to have done me

much good," he observed. "Let me have something to eat. We can then start at once. Get my bag ready."

"What for?"

"And your own," he continued. "We start at once."

My horror may be conceived. The very idea of going down to the center of the earth was simply absurd. I determined therefore to argue the point after dinner.

My uncle's rage was now directed against the cook for having no dinner ready. My explanation, however, satisfied him. He gave her the key, and she soon managed to get sufficient food to satisfy our voracious appetites.

"Harry," he said, in a soft and winning voice, "I have always believed you ingenious, and you have rendered me a service never to be forgotten. Without you, this great discovery would never have been made. It is my duty, therefore, to insist on your sharing the glory."

"He is in a good humor," I thought. "I'll soon let him know my opinion of glory."

"In the first place," he continued, "you must keep the whole affair a secret. There is no more envious race of men than scientific discoverers. Many would start on the same journey."

"I doubt if you would have many competitors," was my reply.

"We should find a perfect stream of pilgrims on the tracks of Arne Saknussemm, if this document were once made public."

"But my dear sir, this paper is very likely a hoax," I urged.

"The book in which we found it is sufficient proof of its authenticity," he replied.

"I will allow that the celebrated professor wrote the lines, but only as a kind of mystification," was my answer.

"We shall see," my uncle remarked with decisive emphasis.

"But what is all this about Yokul, and Sneffels, and Scartaris? I have never heard anything about them."

"The very point to which I am coming. Take down the third atlas from the second shelf, series Z, plate 4."

I went to the shelf and presently returned with the volume indicated.

"This," said my uncle, "is one of the best maps of Iceland. I believe it will settle all your doubts and objections."

With a grim hope to the contrary, I bent over the map.

We Start on a Journey

"You see, the whole island is composed of volcanoes," said the professor, "and note that they all bear the name of Yokul. The word is Icelandic, and means a glacier. In most of the lofty mountains of that region the volcanic eruptions come forth from ice-bound caverns. Hence the name is applied to every volcano on this extraordinary island."

"But what does this word Sneffels mean?"

To this question I expected no rational answer. I was mistaken.

"Follow my finger to the western coast of Iceland; there you see Reykjavik, its capital. Follow the direction of one of its innumerable fjords and what do you see below the sixty-fifth degree of latitude?"

"A peninsula — very like a thighbone in shape."

"And in the center of it — "

"A mountain."

"Well, that's Sneffels."

I had nothing to say.

"That is Sneffels — a mountain about five thousand feet in height, one of the most remarkable on the whole island. And fated to be the most celebrated in the world, for through its crater we shall reach the center of the earth."

"Impossible!" I cried.

"Why impossible?" said Professor Hardwigg in his severest tones.

"Because its crater is choked with lava, with burning rocks — with infinite dangers."

"But if it is extinct?"

"That would make a difference."

"Of course it would. There are about three hundred volcanoes on the whole surface of the globe — but the greater number are extinct. Of these, Sneffels is one. No eruption has occurred since 1219. In fact, it has ceased to be a volcano at all."

I thought of another objection.

"But what is all this about Scartaris and the kalends of July?"

My uncle reflected deeply.

"What appears obscure to you, is clear to me. The Sneffels mountain has many craters.

26

Saknussemm is careful therefore to note the exact one which is the highway into the interior of the earth. He lets us know that about the end of the month of June, the shadow of Mount Scartaris falls upon this one crater. There can be no doubt about this."

My uncle had an answer for everything.

"I accept all your explanations," I said. "And Saknussemm is right. He found the entrance to the bowels of the earth. But it is madness to suppose that he or anyone else ever followed up the discovery."

"Why so, young man?"

"All scientific teaching, theoretical and practical, shows it to be impossible."

"I care nothing for theories," retorted my uncle.

"But is it not well known that heat increases one degree for every seventy feet you descend into the earth? Gold, platinum, even the hardest rocks are in a state of fusion. What would become of us?"

"Don't be alarmed my boy."

"Why so?"

"Neither you nor anybody else knows anything about the real state of the earth's interior. All modern experiments tend to explore older theories. Were any such heat to

27

exist, the upper crust of the earth would be shattered to atoms, and the world would be at an end."

After a long, learned, interesting discussion — my uncle gave his opinion.

"I do not believe in the dangers and difficulties which you, Harry, seem to multiply; and the only way to learn is, like Arne Saknussemm, to go and see."

"Well," I cried, overcome at last, "let us go and see. Though how we can do that in the dark is another mystery."

"Fear nothing. We shall overcome these and many other difficulties. Besides, as we approach the center, I expect to find it luminous — "

"Nothing is impossible."

"And now that we have come to a thorough understanding, not a word to any living soul. Our success depends on secrecy and dispatch."

Leaving my uncle, I went out of the house like one possessed. Was all I had heard really and truly possible? Was my uncle in his sober senses, and could the interior of the earth be reached? Was I the victim of a madman, or was he a discoverer of rare courage and vision?

Afraid my enthusiasm would cool, I determined to go home and pack at once. However, on my way I found that my feelings changed.

"I'm all confused," I cried. "It is a nightmare — I must have dreamed it."

At this moment I came face to face with Gretchen, whom I warmly embraced.

"So you have come to meet me," she said. "How good of you. But what is the matter?"

I told her all. She listened, and for some minutes she could not speak.

"Well?" I said at last, rather anxiously.

"What a magnificent journey. If I were only a man!"

"My dear Gretchen, I thought you would be the first to cry out against this mad enterprise."

"No! On the contrary, I glory in it. It is magnificent, splendid. Harry Lawson, I envy you."

This was the final blow.

When we entered the house we found my uncle surrounded by workmen and porters, who were already packing up. He was pulling and hauling at a bell.

"Where have you been wasting your time? Your bag is not packed, my papers are not in order, the tailor has not brought my clothes, the key of my carpetbag is gone."

I looked at him stupefied. And still he tugged away at the bell.

"We are really off, then?" I said.

"Yes, of course — and you go out for a stroll!"

"When do we go?"

"The day after tomorrow, at daybreak."

I heard no more but darted off to my bedroom and locked myself in. There was no doubt about it now. My uncle had been hard at work all the afternoon. The garden was full of ropes, rope ladders, torches, gourds, iron clamps, crowbars, alpenstocks, and pickaxes — enough to load ten men.

I passed a terrible night. I was called early the next morning to learn that my uncle's decision was unchanged. I also found Gretchen as excited on the subject as her godfather.

Next day, at five o'clock in the morning, the carriage was at the door. Gretchen and the old cook received the keys of the house. Scarcely pausing to wish anyone good-bye, we started on our journey to the center of the earth.

At Alton, a suburb of Hamburg, is the chief station of the Kiel railway. Twenty minutes from the moment of our departure, our carriage entered the station. Our heavy luggage was taken out, weighed, labeled, and placed in a huge van. We then took our tickets, and at exactly seven o'clock were seated opposite each other in a first-class railway carriage.

My uncle said nothing. He was too busy examining his papers, among which of course was the famous parchment, and letters of introduction from the Danish consul which were to pave the way to an introduction to the governor of Iceland. In three hours we reached Kiel, and our baggage was at once transferred to the steamer.

We had the rest of the day before us, a delay of about ten hours which put my uncle in a towering rage. At length, however, we went on board. It was a dark night with a strong breeze and a rough sea; nothing was visible but occasional fires on shore, and here and there a lighthouse. At seven in the morning we arrived at Korsor in Denmark.

Here we took another railway, which in three hours brought us to the capital, Copenhagen, where my uncle hurried out to present one of his letters of introduction. It was to the director of the Museum of Antiquities. Having been informed that we were tourists bound for Iceland, he did all he could to assist us. One wretched hope sustained me now. Perhaps there was no vessel bound for that distant island.

Alas! a little Danish schooner, the *Valkyrie*, was to sail on the second of June for Reykjavik. The captain, Mr. Bjarne, was on board, and was rather surprised at the energy and cordiality with which my uncle shook him by the hand. To him a voyage to Iceland was merely a matter of course. My uncle, on the other hand, considered the event of sublime importance. The sailor took advantage of his enthusiasm to double the fare.

"On Tuesday morning at seven o'clock be on board," said Mr. Bjarne, handing us our receipts.

"Excellent! Glorious!" remarked my uncle, as we sat down to a late breakfast. "Refresh yourself, my boy, and we will take a run through the town."

Our Voyage to Iceland

The hour of departure came at last. My uncle had the most cordial letters of introduction for Baron Trampe, governor of Iceland, for Mr. Pictursson, coadjutor to the bishop, and for Mr. Finsen, mayor of the town of Reykjavik.

On the second of June our precious cargo of luggage was taken on board the *Valkyrie*. We followed, and were shown by the captain to a small cabin with two standing beds, neither very comfortable.

"Well, and have we a fair wind?" cried my uncle, in his most mellifluous accents.

"An excellent wind!" replied Captain Bjarne.

A few minutes afterward, the schooner

started before the wind, under all the canvas she could carry, and entered the channel. An hour later, the capital of Denmark seemed to sink into the waves.

Along the Swedish coast the schooner began to feel the breezes of the Cattegat in earnest. The *Valkyrie* was swift enough, but with all sailing boats there is the same uncertainty.

"How long will the voyage last?" asked my uncle.

"Well, I should think about ten days," replied the skipper, "unless we meet with some northeast gales among the Faroe Islands."

"At all events, there will be no very considerable delay," cried the impatient professor.

"No, Mr. Hardwigg," said the captain, "no fear of that."

Toward evening the schooner doubled Cape Skagen, the northernmost part of Denmark, crossed the Skager-Rak during the night, skirted the extreme point of Norway, and then reached the northern seas. Two days later, we were not far from the coast of Scotland, somewhere near what Danish sailors call Peterhead, and then the *Valkyrie* stretched out direct for the Faroe Islands, between Orkney and Shetland. Our vessel now felt the full force of the ocean waves and the shifting wind. With great difficulty we made the Faroe Isles, and on the eighth day headed direct for Portland, a cape on the southern shores of Iceland.

My uncle, to his great annoyance and shame, was seasick! His time was spent lying in bed, groaning, and wishing for the end of the voyage. I didn't pity him.

On the eleventh day we sighted Cape Portland, over which towered Mount Nyrdals Yokul. The *Valkyrie* kept off the coast, steering to the westward. On all sides were to be seen whole schools of whales and sharks.

My uncle was unable to even crawl on deck, and thus lost the first view of the Land of Promise. Forty-eight hours later, after a storm which drove us far to sea, we were boarded by a pilot. After three hours of dangerous navigation, he brought the schooner safely to anchor in the bay of Faxa before Reykjavik.

My uncle came out of his cabin, pale, haggard, thin, but full of enthusiasm. Nearly the whole population of the town was on foot to see us land.

Professor Hardwigg led me to the quarterdeck of the schooner and pointed inland to a high two-peaked mountain — a double cone covered with eternal snow.

"Behold," he whispered in an awe-stricken voice, "behold — Mount Sneffels!"

Then he descended into the small boat which awaited us. I followed, and in a few minutes we stood upon the soil of mysterious Iceland!

My uncle was most graciously received by the governor of the island, Baron Trampe, by the mayor, and by Mr. Fridriksson, professor of natural science in the college of Reykjavik.

A man of invaluable ability, this modest scholar spoke no languages save Icelandic and Latin. But when he addressed himself to me in Latin, we at once understood one another. He was the only person that I *did* thoroughly understand during the whole period of my residence in this island.

Out of the three rooms in his house, two were placed at our service. In a few hours we were installed with all our baggage.

"Now, Harry," said my uncle, rubbing his hands, "the worst difficulty is over."

"How is the worst difficulty over?" I cried in fresh amazement.

"Here we are in Iceland. Nothing more remains but to descend into the bowels of the earth."

"Well, sir, that is true. But I want to know how we are to get up again."

"That is the least part of the business. It does not worry me. Now, I want to visit the public library. I may find some of Saknussemm's manuscripts there."

"In the meanwhile," I replied, "I will take a walk through the town."

It was not easy to get lost in the two streets of Reykjavik; I had therefore no need to ask my way. The town lies on a flat and marshy plain, between two hills. A vast field of lava skirts it on one side, falling away in terraces toward the sea. On the other side is the large bay of Faxa, bordered on the north by the enormous glacier of Sneffels.

In the center of the new commercial street, I found the public cemetery, enclosed by an earthen wall. I went to the house of the governor — a mere hut in comparison with the Mansion House at Hamburg, but a palace alongside the other Icelandic houses. Between the little lake and the town was the church, and on a rise nearby was the national school, in which were taught Hebrew, English, French, and Danish.

My general impression was of sadness. No

trees, no vegetation — on all sides volcanic peaks. The huts of turf and earth looked more like roofs than houses. Thanks to the heat of these residences, grass grows on the roofs; this grass is carefully cut for hay. I saw but few inhabitants, but I met a crowd on the beach, drying, salting, and loading codfish, the principal export. The men appeared robust, but heavy and fair-haired.

Conversation and Discovery

When I returned, dinner was ready. The meal, which was more Danish than Icelandic, was in itself nothing, but the hospitality of our host made it enjoyable.

Mr. Fridriksson asked my uncle what he thought of the public library.

"Library, sir?" cried my uncle. "It appears to me to be a collection of useless, odd volumes, and a vast amount of empty shelves."

"What!" cried Mr. Fridriksson. "Why we have eight thousand volumes of the most rare and valuable works."

"Eight thousand volumes! My dear sir, where are they?" cried my uncle.

"Scattered over the country, Professor Hardwigg. We think that books should be distributed as widely as possible. The books of our library pass from hand to hand without returning to the library shelves perhaps for years."

"But then when foreigners visit you, there is nothing for them to see."

"If you will tell me what books you expected to find, perhaps I may be able to assist you."

I watched my uncle keenly. For a minute or two he hesitated, as if unwilling to speak. To speak openly might reveal his project. After some reflection, he spoke.

"Well, Mr. Fridriksson," he said, in an easy, unconcerned kind of way. "I was wondering if you had any works of the learned Arne Saknussemm."

"Arne Saknussemm!" cried the professor of Reykjavik. "You speak of one of the most distinguished men of Icelandic science and literature."

"Yes, sir. All that is true, but his works?"

"We have none of them."

"Not in Iceland?"

"In Iceland or elsewhere," answered the other, sadly.

"Why so?"

"Because Arne Saknussemm was persecuted for heresy. In 1573 his works were publicly burnt at Copenhagen at the hands of the common hangman."

"Very good!" murmured my uncle, to the great astonishment of the worthy Icelander.

"What! sir — "

"Yes, yes, all is clear. I now understand why Arne Saknussemm was forced to hide his magnificent discovery . . . was compelled to conceal, beneath the veil of an incomprehensible cryptograph, the secret — "

"What secret?"

"A secret — which — " stammered my uncle.

"Have you discovered some wonderful manuscript?" cried Mr. Fridriksson.

"No, no, I was carried away by my enthusiasm. A mere supposition."

"Oh, I see, sir. Now, to turn to another subject, I hope you will not leave our island without examining its mineralogical riches."

"Well, the fact is, I am rather late. So many learned men have been here before me."

"Yes, but you have no idea how many unknown mountains, glaciers, and volcanoes remain to be studied. From where we sit, I can show you one. There on the edge of the horizon you can see Sneffels."

"Oh, yes, Sneffels," said my uncle.

"One of the most curious volcanoes in existence. The crater has rarely been visited."

"Extinct?"

"Extinct these six hundred years," was the ready reply.

"Well," said my uncle, "I have a great mind to begin my studies with an examination of the geological mysteries of this Mount Seffel — Feisel — what did you call it?"

"Sneffels, my dear sir."

This conversation took place in Latin, and I therefore understood all that had been said. I could scarcely believe my ears — to find my uncle so cunning!

"Yes, yes," he continued, "your proposition delights me. I will climb the summit of Sneffels, and, if possible, will descend into its crater."

"I very much regret," continued Mr. Fridriksson, "that my work will not allow me to accompany you."

"No, no," cried my uncle. "I do not wish to bother you. I thank you, however, with all my heart."

"How do you propose to get to Sneffels?" continued the Icelander.

"By sea. I shall cross the bay. That is the most rapid route."

"Yes, but it cannot be done. We do not have an available boat in Reykjavik. You must go by land along the coast. It is longer, but much more interesting."

"Then I must have a guide."

"Of course, and I have the very man."

"Somebody on whom I can depend?"

"Yes, an inhabitant of the peninsula on which Sneffels is situated. He is a very shrewd and worthy man, with whom you will be well pleased. He speaks Danish like a Dane."

"Can I see him — today?"

"No, tomorrow. He will not be here before."

"Tomorrow then," replied my uncle, with a deep sigh.

Off at Last

That evening I took a brief walk on the shore near Reykjavik, after which I returned to an early sleep. When I awoke I heard my uncle speaking loudly in the next room. I rose hastily and joined him. He was talking in Danish with a man of Herculean build and apparently great strength. His eyes looked quick and intelligent. Very long hair, exceedingly red, fell over his shoulders.

Everything in this man's manner revealed a calm temperament. There was nothing indolent about him, but his appearance spoke of tranquility.

I began to understand his character, simply from the way in which he listened to the wild and impassioned speech of my uncle. While the professor spoke sentence after sentence, he stood with folded arms. When

44

he wanted to say no, he moved his head from left to right. When he agreed he nodded ever so slightly.

This grave silent person was named Hans Bjelke, the man whom Mr. Fridriksson had recommended. He was to be our future guide. Had I sought the world over, I could not have found a greater contradiction to my impulsive uncle.

The plan was that he was to take us to the village of Stapi, at the foot of the volcano. He told us the distance was about twenty-two miles.

When my uncle understood that they were Danish miles, of eight thousand yards each, he was obliged to be more moderate in his plans. Considering the horrible roads we had to follow, he allowed eight to ten days for the journey.

Four horses were prepared for us, two to carry the baggage, and two for myself and my uncle. Hans declared that nothing would ever make him climb on the back of any animal. He knew every inch of that part of the coast, and promised to take us the shortest way.

He was further to remain in my uncle's service during the whole time required for the completion of our scientific investigations.

He was to be paid at the fixed salary of three rix-dollars a week. One stipulation, however, was made by the guide; the money was to be paid to him every Saturday night. Failing this, his engagement was at an end.

The treaty concluded, our worthy guide retired without another word.

"A splendid fellow," said my uncle. "Only he little suspects the marvelous part he is about to play in the history of the world."

"You mean that he should accompany us?"

"To the interior of the earth, yes," replied my uncle. "Why not?"

There were yet forty-eight hours before we could make a start. Our whole time was devoted to packing every object in the most advantageous manner. There were four separate groups. The instruments, the arms, the tools, and the provisions.

The instruments were of course of the best manufacture:

1. A centigrade thermometer, measuring up to 150° (302° Fahrenheit) — which to my mind did not appear half enough — or too much. If the degree of heat in the center of the earth was to rise even half that high we should certainly be cooked. Yet if we wanted

to learn the exact temperature of springs or metal in a state of fusion, it was not enough.

2. A manometer to ascertain the atmospheric pressure. A common barometer perhaps would not have done as well, the atmospheric pressure being likely to increase in proportion as we descended below the surface of the earth.

3. A first-class chronometer made by Boissonnas, of Geneva, set at the meridian of Hamburg from which Germans calculate time, as the English do from Greenwich.

4. Two compasses, one for horizontal guidance, the other to ascertain the dip.

5. A night glass, or binocular telescope, so that we might be able to see objects at night.

6. Two Ruhmkorf's coils which, by means of a curent of electricity, would ensure us a very excellent, easily carried, and certain means of obtaining light.

7. A voltaic battery on the newest principle.

Our arms consisted of two rifles and two revolving six-shooters. Why these were included it was impossible for me to say. I had every reason to believe that we had neither wild beasts nor savages to fear. My uncle, on the other hand, was quite as devoted to his arsenal as to his collection of instruments.

Our tools consisted of two pickaxes, two crowbars, a rope ladder, three iron-shod Alpine poles, a hatchet, a hammer, a dozen wedges, some pointed pieces of iron, and a quantity of strong rope. The whole made a sizable parcel, for the ladder itself was three hundred feet long!

Then there came the important question of provisions. The hamper was not very large, but satisfactory, for I knew that there was enough concentrated essence of meat and biscuit to last six months. The only liquid provided by my uncle was schiedam, a kind of gin. Of water, not a drop. We had, however, an ample supply of gourds, and my uncle counted on finding water, and enough to fill them, as soon as we commenced our downward journey.

We carried a medicine and surgical chest with all apparatus necessary for wounds, fractures, and blows. My uncle had also been careful to lay in a good supply of tobacco, several flasks of very fine gunpowder, boxes of tinder, and a large belt crammed full of notes and gold. Six good boots, rendered watertight, were to be found in the toolbox.

"My boy, with such clothing and such gen-

eral equipment," said my uncle, "we may
hope to travel far."

It took a whole day to put all these in order. In the evening we dined with Baron
Trampe, in company with the mayor of Reykjavik, and Doctor Hyaltalin, the great med-
ical man of Iceland. Mr. Fridriksson was not
present, since he and the governor did not
agree on some matters. In consequence I did
not understand a word that was said at dinner, for my uncle never left off speaking
Icelandic.

The next day our host delighted my uncle
by giving him a good map of Iceland, a most
important and precious document for a min-
eralogist.

Our last evening was spent in a long conversation with Mr. Fridriksson, whom I
liked very much — the more so, since I never
expected to see him, or anyone else for that
matter, again. After this, I tried to sleep.
My night was miserable.

At five o'clock in the morning I was
awakened from the only real half-hour's sleep
of the night, by the loud neighing of horses
under my window.

At six o'clock all our preparations were
completed and Mr. Fridriksson shook hands
heartily with us. My uncle thanked him
warmly for his kind hospitality.

As for myself, I put together a few of my best Latin phrases, and paid him the highest compliment I could.

As we mounted our horses and started off, Mr. Fridriksson called after me in the words of Virgil — words which appeared to have been made for us:

"Et quamcumque viam dederit fortuna sequamur."

("And whichsoever way thou goest, may fortune follow!")

Our Start—We Meet with Adventures by the Way

The weather was overcast when we commenced our perilous journey. Riding through an unknown country was particularly agreeable to me. I began to enjoy the exhilarating delight of traveling. My spirits rose so rapidly that I began to see our journey differently.

"After all," I said to myself, "what do I risk? Simply to take a journey through a curious country, to climb a remarkable mountain, and if the worst comes to the worst to descend into the crater of an extinct volcano."

There could be no doubt that this was all Saknussemm had done. As for the existence of a gallery or subterraneous passage leading into the interior of the earth, the idea was simply absurd. All that may be required of me I will do cheerfully, and will create no difficulty.

Hans, our guide, went first, walking with rapid, unvarying steps. Our two horses with the luggage followed. My uncle and I followed on our horses.

From Reykjavik, Hans had followed the line of the sea. Our horses, appeared not only well acquainted with the country, but by a kind of instinct knew which was the best road.

"I assure you, Harry," my uncle cried, "I begin to think no animal is more intelligent than an Icelandic horse. Between us we shall do our ten leagues a day."

"We may do so," was my reply, "but what about our guide?"

"I have no anxiety about Hans. Look at him. He wastes so little motion that it is impossible for him to become fatigued."

All this while we were advancing at a rapid pace. After traveling fully half a Danish mile, we had met neither a farmer at the door of his hut, nor even a wandering shepherd. We avoided a good deal of rough country by following the winding and desolate shores of the sea.

Some two hours after we had left the city of Reykjavik, we reached the little town called Aoalkirkja, which means "principal church." It consists simply of a few houses — not what in England or Germany we should call a hamlet.

Hans stopped here one half hour. He shared our frugal breakfast, answered yes and no to my uncle's questions, and when asked where we were to pass the night, was as laconic as usual.

"Gardar!" was his one word reply.

Three hours later, we entered Ejulberg. Here the horses were allowed to take some rest and refreshment before going on to Saurboer Annexia, situated on the southern bank of the Hvalfjord.

It was four o'clock in the evening and we had traveled four Danish miles, about equal to twenty English miles. The fjord here was about half a mile wide. The sweeping and broken waves came rolling in upon the pointed rocks.

To ride over this stormy salt water on the back of a little horse seemed to me absurd. But my uncle was in no humor to wait. He dug his heels into the sides of his steed, and made for the shore. His horse went to the very edge of the water, sniffed at the approaching wave, and retreated.

"Wretched animal!" cried my uncle.

"Farja," said the guide, tapping him on the shoulder.

"What, a ferryboat!"

"Der," answered Hans, pointing to the boat in question.

"Why did you not say so before?" cried my uncle. "Why not start at once?"

"Tidvatten," said the guide.

"What does he say?" I asked, considerably puzzled by the dialogue.

"He says tide," replied my uncle, translating the Danish word.

"Of course I understand — we must wait till the tide serves."

My uncle frowned, and followed the horses to where the boat lay.

I understood the necessity for waiting before crossing the fjord until that moment when the sea, at its highest point, is in a state of slack water. The ferryboat was then in no danger of being carried out to sea, or dashed on the rocky coast.

The favorable moment came at six o'clock in the evening. Then my uncle, myself, Hans, two boatmen, and the four horses got into a very awkward flat-bottom boat. After the steam ferryboats of the Elbe, I found the long oars of the boatmen a sorry means of locomotion, but half an hour later we reached Gardar.

Traveling in Iceland— the Lepers

The nocturnal illumination did not surprise me, for in Iceland during the months of June and July the sun never sets.

The temperature, however, was much lower than I expected. I was cold and ravenously hungry. The hut which hospitably opened its doors to us was welcome indeed.

It was the house of a peasant, but in hospitality it was the palace of a king. At the door the master of the house came forward, held out his hand, and signaled us to follow him.

We followed him through a long, narrow, gloomy passage. This passage opened into every room, four in number: the kitchen; the workshop, where the weaving was carried on; the general sleeping chamber of the family; and the best room, to which strangers were especially invited.

Our chamber was a large room with a hard earthen floor, lighted by a window with panes made of the intestines of sheep — very far from transparent.

The bed was made of dry hay thrown into two long red wooden boxes. There was one objection to the house, the powerful odor of dried fish, of macerated meat, and of sour milk.

As soon as we had taken off our heavy traveling clothes, our host called us into the kitchen, the only room in which the Icelanders ever make any fire, no matter how cold it may be.

A large stone standing in the middle of the hard earthen floor was the fireplace; above, in the roof, was a hole for the smoke to pass through. This room was kitchen, parlor, and dining room all in one.

On our entrance, our host, as if he had not seen us before, advanced ceremoniously, uttered the word *soellvertu*, which means "be happy," and then kissed both of us on the cheek.

His wife followed, pronounced the same word with the same ceremonial, then the husband and wife, placing their right hands upon their hearts, bowed.

This excellent Icelandic woman was the mother of nineteen children, who, little and big, rolled, crawled, and walked about in the midst of volumes of smoke arising from the angular fireplace. Every now and then I would see another towhead or a slightly melancholy face, peering at me through the smoke.

Both my uncle and myself were very friendly with the whole party, and before long there were three or four of these little ones on our shoulders or hanging about our legs. Those who could speak kept crying out *soellvertu* in every possible and impossible key.

Supper was announced and at this moment our guide came in after setting the horses loose to browse on the stunted green of the Icelandic prairies. There was little for them to eat but moss and some very dry grass.

"Welcome," said Hans.

Then, tranquilly, he embraced the host and hostess and their nineteen children.

This ceremony concluded, we all sat down to table, twenty-four of us — somewhat crowded. Those who were best off had only two juveniles on their knees.

Our host filled our plates with a portion of lichen soup, and an enormous lump of fish floating in sour butter. After that there came some *skyr*, a kind of curds and whey, served with biscuits and juniper-berry juice. For drink, we had *blanda*, skimmed milk with water. I was still hungry; I finished up with a basin of thick oaten porridge.

As soon as the meal was over, the children disappeared, whilst the grownups sat around the fireplace, on which was placed turf, heather, cow dung and dried fish bones. When everybody was sufficiently warm, all retired to their respective beds.

Next day, at five in the morning, we took our leave of these hospitable people. My uncle had great difficulty making them accept a sufficient remuneration.

Hans then gave the signal to start.

Scarcely a hundred yards from Gardar, the character of the country changed. The soil became marshy and boggy. To the right, the range of mountains was like a great system of natural fortifications. We forded numerous streams and rivulets. As we advanced, the deserted appearance increased, yet now and then we could see human shadows in the distance. The unhappy wretches never came forward to beg; on the contrary, they ran away. Not, however, before Hans was able to salute them with the universal *soellvertu.*

"*Spetelsk,*" said he.

"A leper," explained my uncle.

The horrible affliction known as leprosy, which has almost vanished through modern science, was common in Iceland.

These poor lepers did not enliven our journey, and the scene was inexpressibly sad and lonely. The very last tufts of grassy vegetation appeared to die at our feet. Not a tree was to be seen, except a few stunted willows about as big as blackberry bushes. I could not suppress a sense of melancholy. I sighed for my own native land, and wished to be back with Gretchen.

We crossed several little fjords, and at last came to a real gulf. The tide was at its height, so we were able to go over at once, and reached the hamlet of Alftanes, about a mile farther.

That evening, after fording two rivers rich in trout and pike, we passed the night in a deserted house. The following night we slept at the Annexia of Krosolbt.

For a whole mile we walked on nothing but lava from the neighboring mountains, all extinct volcanoes. Here and there we could see steam from hot-water springs.

There was no time for us to take more than a cursory view of these phenomena. We had to go forward with all speed. We had, in fact, swept around the great bay of Faxa, and the twin white summits of Sneffels rose to the clouds at a distance of less than five miles.

The horses now advanced rapidly; the difficulty of the soil no longer checked them. Fatigue began to tell upon me, but my uncle was as fresh as he had been on the first day. Both the professor and the guide appeared to regard this rugged expedition as a mere walk!

On Saturday, June 20th, at six o'clock in the evening, we reached Budir, a small town on the ocean shore. Here the guide asked for his money. My uncle settled with him immediately. It was now the family of Hans himself, that is to say his uncles and cousins, who offered us hospitality. We were exceedingly well received, and I should have liked very much to have rested with them. But my uncle did not require rest, and despite the fact that the next day was Sunday, I was compelled once more to mount my horse.

We were now skirting the enormous base

of the mighty volcano. My uncle never took his eyes off it; he could not keep from looking at it with a kind of defiance, as if to say, "This is the giant I have made up my mind to conquer."

After four hours of steady traveling, the horses stopped of themselves before the door of the presbytery of Stapi.

We Reach Mount Sneffels

Stapi consists of thirty huts, built on a large plain of lava. Its humble homes stretch along the end of the little fjord, surrounded by a basaltic wall.

Basalt is a brown rock of igneous origin. It assumes astonishing forms here, a severe order of architecture to equal the splendors of Babylon and the marvels of Greece.

This was the last stage of our journey. Hans had brought us along with fidelity and intelligence. I began to feel more comfortable when I reflected that he was to accompany us still farther on our way.

When we halted before the house of the rector, a small cabin no better than those of his neighbors, I saw a man in the act of shoeing a horse, a hammer in his hand and a leather apron tied around his waist.

"Be happy," said Hans, in his own language.

"*Good-dag!*" ("good day!") replied the former, in excellent Danish.

"*Kyrkoherde,*" cried Hans, turning round and introducing him to my uncle.

"The rector," repeated the professor. "It appears, my dear Harry, the rector is not above doing his own work."

Hans explained to the Kyrkoherde who we were. The man gave a kind of halloo, upon which a tall woman, almost a giantess, came out of the hut. She was at least six feet high.

My first impression of her was one of horror. I thought she had come to give us the Icelandic kiss. I had nothing to fear, for she did not even show much willingness to receive us into her house.

The room set aside for strangers appeared to me to be by far the worst room in the presbytery. The rector did not practice the usual Icelandic hospitality. Before the day was over, I found we were dealing with a blacksmith, a fisherman, a hunter, a carpenter, anything but a clergyman. It must be said that we had caught the rector on a weekday; probably he appeared to greater advantage on the Sunday.

Fortunately, preparations for our departure were made the very next day after our arrival at Stapi. Hans now hired two Icelanders to take the place of the horses, which could no longer carry our luggage. When we had reached the bottom of the crater, the two men were to leave us. This point was settled before they agreed to start.

My uncle took this occasion to partially confide in Hans that it was his intention to continue his exploration of the volcano to the last possible limit.

Hans listened calmly, and then nodded his head. To bury himself in the bowels of the earth or to travel over its summits, it was all the same to him! Amused and occupied by the incidents of travel I had begun to forget the future. But now I once more realized the actual state of affairs. What was to be done? Run away? If I really had intended to leave Professor Hardwigg to his fate, it should have been at Hamburg and not at the foot of Sneffels.

One terrible idea above all others began to trouble me.

"Let us consider," I said to myself. "We are going to climb the Sneffels mountain. Well and good. We are about to pay a visit to the very bottom of the crater. Still good.

"That, however, is not the whole matter. If a road does exist into the dark and subterraneous bowels of Mother Earth, we shall be in the midst of the volcano. Now, we have no evidence to prove that Sneffels is really extinct. Because the monster has slept soundly since 1219, does it follow that it is never to awake?"

I reflected long and deeply. The more I thought, the more I objected to being reduced to ashes. At last I determined to submit the case to my uncle, and lay my fears before him.

"I have been thinking about the matter," he said in the quietest tone in the world.

Was he at last about to listen to the voice of reason? It was almost too good to be true. I allowed him to reflect at his leisure. After some moments he spoke out.

"I have been thinking about the matter," he repeated. "Ever since we arrived at Stapi, my mind has been full of the grave questions which you submitted to me. Nothing would be worse than to act with imprudence."

"I heartily agree with you, dear Uncle."

"It is now six hundred years since Sneffels has spoken. I have talked to the inhabitants of this region. I have carefully studied the soil, and I tell you emphatically, my dear

Harry, there will be no eruption in the near future."

I was stupefied.

"I see you doubt my word," said my uncle. "Follow me."

I obeyed mechanically.

Leaving the presbytery, the professor took a road which led away from the sea. We were soon in the open country. The whole land seemed crushed under the weight of enormous stones — of trap, of basalt, of granite, of lava, and of all other volcanic substances.

I could see many spouts of steam rising in the air. These white vapors, called in the Icelandic language *reykir*, come from hot-water fountains, and indicate by their violence the volcanic activity of the soil. The sight of these appeared to justify my apprehension. My uncle addressed me.

"You see all this smoke, Harry, my boy?"

"Yes, sir."

"Well, as long as they are like this, you have nothing to fear from the volcano."

"How can that be?"

"At the approach of an eruption these spouts of vapor redouble their activity, then disappear altogether during the period of volcanic eruption. For the elastic fluids seek refuge in the interior of the crater, instead of escaping through the fissures of the earth. If, then, the steam remains in its normal state and the wind is not replaced by heavy atmospheric pressure and dead calm, you may be quite sure that there is no fear of any immediate eruption."

"But — "

"Enough, my dear boy. When science has sent forth her command, it is only to hear and obey."

I came back to the house quite downcast. My uncle's scientific arguments had completely defeated me. Nevertheless, I hoped that once we were at the bottom of the crater it would be impossible to descend any deeper, despite all the learned Saknussemms in the world.

It was now June 23rd. Hans was awaiting us outside the presbytery with his two companions, loaded with provisions, tools, and instruments. Hans had added to our baggage a large skinful of water. This assured us water for eight days.

By nine o'clock in the morning we were ready. The rector and his huge wife or servant, I never knew which, stood at the door to see us off. Instead of the usual kiss of the Icelanders, their adieu took the shape of a formidable bill, in which they even included the use of the pastoral house, really and truly the most abominable place I ever was in.

My uncle paid without bargaining. A man who had made up his mind to undertake a voyage into the interior of the earth is not the man to haggle over a few rix-dollars.

Hans gave the signal and some few moments later we had left Stapi.

The Ascent of Mount Sneffels

The huge volcano which was the first stage of our daring experiment is about five thousand feet high. Sneffels is the termination of a long range of volcanic mountains and one of its peculiarities is its two huge pointed summits.

The commencement of the great undertaking filled me with awe. Now that we had actually started, I began to believe in the reality of the undertaking!

We walked in single file. Hans led us by paths where two persons could not walk abreast. We had all the more opportunity to reflect on the awful grandeur of the scene around.

Beyond the extraordinary basaltic wall of the fjord of Stapi we found ourselves making our way across fibrous turf, the residue of ancient vegetation of a swampy peninsula.

As a true nephew of the great Professor

Hardwigg, I observed this vast museum of natural history with great interest.

This extraordinary and curious island must have made its appearance at a comparatively recent date. Like the coral islands of the Pacific, it may, for all we know, be still rising by slow and imperceptible degrees.

If this really is the case, its origin can be attributed to only one cause — the continued action of subterranean fires.

If so, away with the theories of Sir Humphrey Davy. Away with the authority of the parchment of Arne Saknussemm, the wonderful pretensions to discovery on the part of my uncle — and to our journey!

All must end in smoke.

Charmed with the idea, I began to look about me more carefully. A serious study of the soil was necessary to negate or confirm my hypothesis.

Iceland, being absolutely without sedimentary soil, is composed exclusively of volcanic tufa: porous stones and rocks. Long before the existence of volcanoes, it was composed of a solid body of massive traprock lifted bodily out of the sea by the action of the centrifugal force at work in the earth.

At a later period in the world's history, a huge fissure must have opened diagonally from the southwest to the northeast of the island, through which by degrees flowed the volcanic lava. The seething fused matter, ejected from the earth, spread slowly to form vast level plains.

At length a time came when, despite the enormous thickness and weight of the upper crust, the mechanical forces of the gases below became so great, that they upheaved the weighty back and made huge, gigantic shafts. Hence the volcanoes which suddenly arose through the upper crust, forming craters at the summit of these new creations.

Thus, the volcanoes gave free passage to the fiery overflow of lava, and to the mass of cinders and pumice stone now scattered over the sides of the mountain.

Here, in a nutshell, I had the whole history of the phenomena from which, I believed, Iceland arose. To believe that its central mass did not remain in a state of liquid fire, white hot, was simply and purely madness.

This being satisfactorily proved, then what folly to pretend to penetrate into the interior of the mighty earth!

This mental lecture did me good. I was now quite certain about the fate of our enterprise, and so proceeded stoically, like a brave soldier mounting a battery.

As we advanced, the road became more difficult, and we had to be scrupulously careful in order to avoid dangerous and constant falls.

Hans advanced as calmly as if he had been walking over Salisbury Plain. If we momentarily lost sight of him, there was a shrill whistle to tell us where he was.

Occasionally he would pile rocks into small heaps *in order that we might not lose our way on our return.*

Three hours of terrible fatigue, walking incessantly, brought us only to the foot of the great mountain.

Suddenly Hans cried a halt — and a kind of breakfast was laid out on the lava before us.

Uncle was so eager to advance that he bolted his food. His guide, however, did not give the signal for departure for a good hour.

From this, our first real stage, we began to ascend the slopes of the Sneffels volcano.

The stones on the mountainside gave way continually under our feet, and went rushing like avalanches onto the plains. Often we were obliged to help each other along by means of our climbing poles.

My uncle stuck as close to me as possible.

He never lost sight of me, and on many occasions his arm supplied me with firm and solid support. He was strong, wiry, and apparently insensible to fatigue. He never slipped or failed in his steps. The Icelanders, though heavily loaded, climbed with the agility of mountaineers.

After an hour of unheard-of fatigue, we came to a vast field of ice called the table-cloth, which wholly surrounded the bottom of the cone of the volcano.

Here, to our surprise, we found an actual flight of stone steps — like everything else, volcanic. It had been formed by one of those torrents of stones cast up by an eruption.

The character of the slopes momentarily increased, but these remarkable stone steps enabled us to proceed.

About seven in the evening of that day, after having clambered up two thousand steps, we found ourselves overlooking a kind of projection of the mountain.

The ocean lay beneath us more than three thousand two hundred feet. We had reached the region of eternal snows.

The cold was keen, searching, intense. The wind blew with extraordinary violence. I was utterly exhausted.

My uncle saw this clearly. Despite his

impatience, he decided, with a sigh, upon a halt. He called Hans to his side. Hans, however, shook his head.

"Ofvanfor," was his sole spoken reply.

"It appears," said my uncle, "that we must go higher."

He turned to Hans, and asked him the reason for this decisive response.

"Mistour," replied the guide.

"Ja mistour," ("yes, the mistour"), cried one of the Icelandic guides in a terrified tone.

It was the first time he had spoken.

"What does this mysterious word signify?" I anxiously inquired.

"Look," said my uncle.

I looked down upon the plain below, and saw a prodigious volume of pulverized pumice stone, sand, and dust rising to the heavens in the form of a mighty waterspout.

The wind was driving it directly toward our side of Sneffels.

If this sand spout broke over us, we would all be destroyed.

"Hastigt!" cried our guide.

I certainly knew nothing of Danish, but I thoroughly understood that he meant us to hurry.

The guide turned rapidly to the back of

the crater, all the while acending slightly.

We followed instantly.

A quarter of an hour later Hans paused to enable us to look back. The mighty whirlwind of sand was spreading up the slope of the mountain to the very spot where we had proposed to halt. Huge stones were caught up, cast into the air, and thrown about as during an eruption. But for the precaution and knowledge of our guide, we would have been cast to the wind like dust from some unknown meteor.

Hans did not think it prudent to pass the night on the outside of the cone. We continued our journey in a zigzag direction. The fifteen hundred feet to the top took us at least five hours. I never felt such misery, fatigue, and exhaustion in my life.

But at last we had reached the summit of Mount Sneffels. Despite my fatigue, before I descended into the crater that was to shelter us for the night, I paused to behold the sunrise at midnight, and enjoyed the spectacle of its ghastly pale rays cast upon the isle which lay sleeping at our feet!

I no longer wondered at people traveling all the way to Norway to behold this wondrous spectacle.

The Shadow of Scartaris

Our supper was eaten rapidly, after which
everybody did the best he could for himself
within the hollow of the crater. The bed was
hard and the shelter uncomfortable — lying
in the open air five thousand feet above the
level of the sea!

Next day we awoke nearly frozen by the
keen air. I left my granite couch to enjoy
the magnificent spectacle at our feet.

From the lofty summit of Mount Sneffel's
southern peak a giant picture stretched out
before us. We could see deep valleys that
crossed each other in every direction, lakes
that seemed no bigger than ponds, and rivers
no bigger than brooks. To my right were
glaciers upon glaciers, and multiplied peaks
topped with light clouds of smoke.

Where the earth ended and the sea began, it was impossible for the eye to distinguish.

I wholly forgot who I was, and where I was.

My uncle, turning to the west, pointed out a kind of haze with a faint outline of land rising out of the waters.

"Greenland!" he said.

"Greenland?" I exclaimed.

"Yes. We are not more than thirty-five leagues distant from that wonderful land." My uncle always spoke as if he were lecturing a class. "We are now on the summit of Sneffels. Here are its two peaks, north and south. Hans will tell you the name by which the people of Iceland call that on which we stand."

The guide nodded and spoke, as usual, one word:

"Scartaris."

My uncle looked at me with a proud and triumphant glance.

"A crater," he said. "You hear?"

I did hear, but I was totally unable to reply.

The crater of Mount Sneffels represented an inverted cone, the gaping top apparently half a mile across, the depth indefinite feet. Conceive what this *hole* must have been like when full of flame and thunder and lightning. The bottom of the funnel-shaped hollow was about five hundred feet in circumference. The slope from the summit to the bottom was very gradual, and we were clearly able to get there without much difficulty.

"To descend into the interior of a cannon," I thought to myself, "when it might be loaded and might go off at the least shock, is the act of a madman."

But there was no longer any opportunity for me to hesitate. Hans, with a perfectly calm and indifferent air, took his usual post at the head of the band.

I felt like a lamb led to the slaughter.

Hans took his way down the interior of the cone in a zigzag fashion, making, as the sailors say, long tracks to the eastward followed by equally long ones to the west.

Many portions of the cone consisted of inferior glaciers. Whenever Hans met with one of these he advanced with caution, sounding the soil with his long iron pole in order to discover fissures and layers of deep soft snow. In many doubtful or dangerous places, we were tied together by a long rope. Should any one of us slip, he would be supported by his companions. Nevertheless, we made considerable progress without accident.

By midday, we were at the end of our journey. I looked upwards and saw only a circular frame to a very small portion of the sky — a portion which seemed to me singularly beautiful. Should I ever again gaze on that lovely sunlit sky?

The bottom of the crater was composed of three separate shafts, through which, when Sneffels was in action, the great central furnace sent forth its burning lava and poisonous vapors. Each of these chimneys, or shafts, gaped open-mouthed in our path. I kept as far away from them as possible, not even venturing to peep downwards.

The professor, after a rapid examination of their disposition and characteristics, became breathless. He ran from one to the other uttering incomprehensible phrases in all languages.

Hans and his humbler companions seated themselves on some piles of lava and looked silently on. They clearly took my uncle for a lunatic.

Suddenly the professor uttered a wild, unearthly cry. At first I imagined he had lost his footing, and was falling headlong into one of the yawning gulfs. Nothing of the kind. I saw him, his arms spread out to their widest extent, his legs stretched apart, standing upright before an enormous pedestal. His attitude was that of a man utterly stupefied. But his stupefaction was speedily changed to the wildest joy.

"Harry! Harry! come here!" he cried. "Make haste! Wonderful — wonderful!"

I turned to obey his commands. Neither Hans nor the other Icelanders moved a step.

"Look!" said the professor.

And fully joining in his stupefaction, if not his joy, I read on the eastern side of the huge block of stone the name that was to me a thousand times accursed.

"Arne Saknussemm!" cried my uncle. "Now, unbeliever, do you begin to have faith?"

Totally unable to speak, I went back to my pile of lava. The evidence was overwhelming!

In a few moments, however, my thoughts were far away, back in my German home with Gretchen and the old cook. What would I have given for one of my cousin's smiles, for one of our ancient domestic's omelets, and for my own feather bed!

Hours later, when I at last raised my head from between my hands, there remained at the bottom of the crater only myself, my uncle, and Hans. The Icelandic porters had been dismissed, and were now descending the exterior slopes of Mount Sneffels on their way back to Stapi.

Hans slept tranquilly at the foot of a rock, in a kind of rill of lava, where he had made himself a rough and ready bed. My uncle was walking about the bottom of the crater like a wild beast in a cage. I seemed both to hear and feel continued heavings and shudderings in the mountain.

In this way we passed our first night in the interior of a crater.

Next morning, a gray, heavy sky hung like a funeral pall over the volcanic cone. I noticed only my uncle's rage.

I fully understood the reason.

Of the three openings which yawned beneath our steps, only one had been followed by Saknussemm — that one that the shadow of Scartaris fell upon, just touching its mouth, in the last days of the month of June.

We were to consider the peak as the stylus of an immense sundial, the shadow of which pointed at a given time to the yawning chasm which led into the interior of the earth.

Now, should the sun fail to appear, no

shadow. Consequently, no chance of discovering the right aperture. We had reached the 25th of June.

It would be utterly impossible to depict the rage of Professor Hardwigg. The day passed away, and not the faintest outline of a shadow could be seen at the bottom of the crater. Hans never moved from his place. My uncle never addressed a word to me; he was nursing his wrath to keep it warm. His eyes fixed on the black and foggy atmosphere. Never had his eyes appeared so fierce.

On the 26th no change for the better. A mixture of rain and snow fell during the whole day. Hans very quietly built himself a hut of lava into which he retired like Diogenes into his tub.

My uncle was almost frantic. To be sure, it was enough to make even a patient man angry. He had reached one goal of his desires, yet was likely to be wrecked in port.

But on Sunday, the last day but one of the month, there came a change of weather. The sun poured its rays to the very bottom of the crater. Each hillock, rock, and stone had its share. To my uncle's insane delight, the shadow of Scartaris was clear, and moved slowly with the radiant sun.

My uncle moved with it in a state of ecstasy.

At twelve o'clock exactly, when the sun had attained its highest altitude for the day, the shadow fell upon the edge of the central pit!

"Here it is," gasped the professor, in an agony of joy. "Here it is — we have found it. Forward, my friends, into the interior of the earth."

I looked curiously at Hans to see what reply he would make to this terrifying announcement.

"*Forut*," said the guide tranquilly.

"Forward it is," answered my uncle, who was now in the seventh heaven of delight.

When we were quite ready, our watches indicated thirteen minutes past one.

The Real Journey Commences

Our real journey had now commenced. Hitherto our courage and determination had overcome all difficulties. We were tired at times, but that was all. Now we were faced by unknown and fearful dangers.

I had not as yet ventured to take a glimpse down the horrible abyss into which I was about to plunge. The fatal moment had, however, at last arrived. Hans seemed to accept the difficulties of the journey so tranquilly that I actually blushed to appear less courageous than he!

Had I been alone with my uncle, I should certainly have sat down and argued the point fully, but in the presence of the guide I held my tongue. I gave a thought to my charming Gretchen, and then I advanced to the mouth of the central shaft.

It measured about a hundred feet in diameter, which made it about three hundred in circumstance. I leaned over a rock which stood on its edge and looked down. My hair stood on end, my teeth chattered, my limbs trembled. There is nothing more powerful than this attraction toward an abyss. I was about to fall headlong into the gaping well when I was drawn back by the firm and powerful hand of Hans.

Few as the minutes were during which I gazed down this tremendous shaft, I had enough of a glimpse to give me some idea of its physical conformation. Its sides, which were almost as perpendicular as those of a well, presented numerous projections which doubtless would assist our descent.

It was a sort of wild and savage staircase, without banister or fence. A rope fastened above, near the surface, would certainly support our weight and enable us to eventually reach the bottom. But when we had arrived at its utmost length, how were we to loosen it above?

My uncle hit upon a very simple method. He unrolled a rope about as thick as my thumb and at least four hundred feet in length. He allowed about half of it to go down the pit, then passed the rope over a great bloc of lava which stood on the edge of the precipice. This done, he let down the second half after the first.

Each of us could now descend to a depth of two hundred feet by catching the two ropes in one hand. All we had to do then was to let go of one end of the rope and pull away at the other. The rope would come falling at our feet. In order to go down farther, all that was necessary was to repeat the same operation.

"Now," said my uncle, "let us see about the baggage. It must be divided into three separate parcels, and each of us must carry one on his back."

"Hans," he continued, "you will take charge of the tools and some of the provisions. You, Harry, must take another third of the provisions, and the arms. I will load myself with the rest of the eatables and with the more delicate instruments."

"But," I exclaimed, "our clothes, this mass of rope and ladders — who will carry them down?"

"They will go down of themselves."

"How so?" I asked.

My uncle was not given to hesitation. He had the whole of the nonfragile articles made up into one bundle and the packet, firmly fastened, was simply pitched over the edge of the gulf.

I heard the moaning of the suddenly displaced air, and the noise of falling stones. My uncle, leaning over the abyss, followed the descent of his luggage with a self-satisfied air, and did not rise until it had completely disappeared from sight.

"Now then," he cried, "it is our turn."

The professor fastened his case of instruments on his back. Hans took charge of the tools, I of the arms. The descent then commenced in the following order: Hans went first, my uncle followed, and I went last. Our progress was made in profound silence — a silence only troubled by the fall of rock, which, breaking from the jagged sides, fell with a roar into the depths below.

I allowed myself to slide, holding onto the double rope with one hand and with the other keeping myself off the rocks with the help of my ironshod pole. I had one fear. The rope appeared to me far too fragile to bear the weight of three such persons as we were with our luggage. I made as little use of it as possible, trusting to my own agility. I performed miraculous feats of dexterity and strength upon the projecting shelves and spurs of lava, which my feet seemed to clutch as strongly as my hands.

In about half an hour we reached a kind of small terrace, formed by a fragment of rock projecting some distance from the sides of the shaft.

Hans now began to haul on the cord on one side only, the other going as quietly upward as the other came down. It fell at last, bringing with it a shower of small stones, lava, and dust.

While we were seated on this extraordinary terrace, I ventured once more to look downwards. With a sigh I discovered that the bottom was still invisible. Were we then going direct to the interior of the earth?

The performance with the rope was repeated, and a quarter of an hour later we had reached to a depth of four hundred feet.

I doubt if the most dedicated geologist would have studied the layers of earth around him during that descent. Yet the inveterate professor, my uncle, must have done so all the way down. For at one of our halts he began a brief lecture.

"The farther we advance," said he, "the greater is my confidence in the result. The disposition of these volcanic strata absolutely confirms the theories of Sir Humphrey Davy. We are still within the regions of the primordial soil. At all events, we shall soon know the truth."

My silence was taken for consent.

At the expiration of three hours we were, to all appearances, as far as ever from the bottom of the well. When I looked upwards, however, I could see that the opening was every minute decreasing in size. The sides of the shaft were getting closer and closer together. We were approaching the regions of eternal night!

And still we continued to descend!

At length, I noticed that when pieces of stone were detached from the sides of this precipice, they were swallowed up with less noise than before. The final sound was sooner heard. We were approaching the bottom of the abyss!

As I had been very careful to keep track of all the changes of rope which took place, I was able to tell exactly the depth we had reached, as well as the time it had taken.

We had shifted the rope twenty-eight times, each operation taking a quarter of an hour, which in all made seven hours. To this had to be added twenty-eight rest periods; in all it took us ten hours and a half. We started at one; it was now therefore about eleven o'clock at night.

It does not require any great knowledge of arithmetic to know that twenty-eight times two hundred feet make five thousand six hundred feet in all — more than an English mile!

While I was making this mental calculation a voice broke the silence. It was the voice of Hans.

"Halt!" he cried.

I checked myself very suddenly; I was about to kick my uncle on the head.

"We have reached the end of our journey," said the professor.

"What, the interior of the earth?" I said, slipping down to his side.

"No, you stupid fellow! But we have reached the bottom of the well."

"And I suppose there is no further progress to be made?" I asked hopefully.

"Oh, yes. I can dimly see a sort of tunnel, which turns off to the right. We must see about that tomorrow. Let us eat now and seek slumber as best we may."

I thought it time.

It was not even now completely dark, the light filtering down in a most extraordinary manner.

We opened the provision bag, ate a frugal supper, and each did his best to find a bed amid the pile of stones, dirt, and lava which had accumulated for ages at the bottom of the shaft.

I stretched myself on the pile of ropes, ladders, and clothes which we had thrown down. After such a day's labor, my rough bed seemed as soft as down!

After lying quietly for some minutes, I opened my eyes and looked upward. I made out a brilliant little dot at the extremity of this long, gigantic telescope.

It was a star without scintillating rays. I calculated it must be in the constellation of the Little Bear, and then dropped into a sound sleep.

We Continue our Descent

At eight o'clock the next morning we awoke. A faint kind of dawn of day greeted us. The thousand and one prisms of the lava reflected the light from above, passing it downward to us. We were able with ease to see objects around us.

"Well, Harry, my boy," cried the delighted professor, rubbing his hands together, "what say you now? Did you ever pass a more tranquil night in our house in the Königstrasse? No deafening sounds of wagon wheels, no cries of hawkers, no bad language from boatmen!"

"Well, Uncle, it was quiet. But to me there is something terrible in this calm."

"Why," said the professor hotly, "one would say you were beginning to be afraid. How will you get on later? We have not yet penetrated one inch into the bowels of the earth."

"What can you mean, sir?" was my astonished reply.

"I mean we have only just reached the soil of the island itself. This long vertical tube, which ends at the bottom of the crater of Sneffels, ceases here at just about sea level."

"Are you sure, sir?"

"Quite sure. Consult the barometer."

It was quite true that the mercury, after rising gradually in the instrument during our descent, had stopped precisely at twenty-nine inches.

"As yet," said the professor, "we have had only to endure the pressure of air. I am curious to replace the barometer with the manometer."

The barometer, in fact, was about to become useless — as soon as the weight of the air became greater than the weight of the air above the level of the ocean.

"But," said I, "this ever-increasing pressure may turn out to be very painful and inconvenient."

"No," he replied, "we shall descend very slowly. Our lungs will gradually become accustomed to breathing compressed air. It is well known that aeronauts have gone so high as to be nearly without air at all. Why should we not accustom ourselves to breathe when we have a little too much of it? Let us not lose a moment. Where is the packet which preceded us in our descent?"

I smilingly pointed it out to my uncle.

"Now," said my uncle, "let us breakfast like people who have a long day's work before them."

Our meal consisted of biscuit and dried meat, washed down by some mouthfuls of water flavored with schiedam.

As soon as we had finished eating, my uncle took from his pocket a notebook destined to be filled by memoranda of our travels. He had already placed his instruments in order, and this was what he wrote:

Monday, July 1st.

Chronometer, 8h. 17m. morning.

Barometer, 29.7 inches.

Thermometer, 6 degrees Centigrade (42.8° Fahrenheit).

Direction, E.S.E.

This last observation was by compass.

"Now, Harry," cried the professor, "we are truly about to take our first step into the interior of the earth — never visited by man since the creation of the world. At this precise moment our travels really commence."

As my uncle made this remark, he took the Ruhmkorf coil apparatus, which hung round his neck, in one hand and with the other he connected the electric current to the coil of the lantern. A bright light at once illumined that dark and gloomy tunnel!

The effect was magical!

Hans, who carried the second apparatus, had it also in operation. These electric beams enabled us to move along by the light of an artificial day, even though we should move amid the most combustible gases.

Each took up his burden. Hans first, my uncle following, and I going third, we entered the somber gallery!

Just as we were about to engulf ourselves in this dismal passage, I lifted up my head and through the tubelike shaft saw that Iceland sky I was never to see again!

Was it the last I should ever see of any sky?

The stream of lava, flowing from the bowels of the earth in 1219, had forced itself through the steep tunnel. It had lined the whole of the inside with its thick and brilliant coating. The electric light added very greatly to the brilliance of the effect.

The great difficulty of our journey now began — how to prevent our slipping down the steeply inclined plain? Happily some cracks, abrasions of the soil, and other irregularities, served as steps. We descended slowly, allowing our heavy luggage to slip on ahead at the end of a long rope.

But that which served as steps under our feet, became in other places stalactites. The lava, very porous in certain places, took the form of little round blisters. Crystals of opaque quartz, adorned with limpid drops of natural glass, suspended to the roof like lustres, seemed to take fire as we passed beneath them.

"Magnificent, glorious!" I cried, in a moment of involuntary enthusiasm. "What a spectacle, uncle! This lava runs through a whole series of colors, from reddish brown to pale yellow — and these crystals, they appear like luminous globes."

"You are beginning to see the charms of travel, Harry," cried my uncle. "Wait a bit, until we advance farther. What we have as yet discovered is nothing!"

We were going down an inclined plain with perfect ease. Nevertheless, to my surprise, we found no perceptible increase in heat. This proved the theories of Humphrey Davy to be true. More than once I found myself examining the thermometer in silent astonishment. Two hours after our departure it registered only 10 degrees Centigrade

(50° Fahrenheit), a difference of only four.

As for discovering the exact depth to which we had attained, nothing could be easier. The professor, as he advanced, measured the angles of deviation and inclination. But he kept the results of his observations to himself.

About eight o'clock in the evening, my uncle gave the signal for halting. The lamps were hung to fissures in the lava rock. We were now in a large airy cavern. What could be the cause of this draft? This was a question I did not care to discuss just then. Fatigue and hunger made me incapable of reasoning.

Hans laid out some provisions on a lump of lava, and we ate with keen relish. One thing, however, caused us great uneasiness — our water reserve was already half exhausted. I called my uncle's attention to our failure to find water.

"We shall find plenty of water — in fact, far more than we shall want," my uncle said.

"But when?"

"When we once get through this crust of lava."

"But what if lava extends to the center of the earth? And as yet I don't think we have gone far in a vertical direction."

"What put that idea into your head?" asked my uncle.

"Well, it appears to me that if we had descended very far below the level of the sea, we should find it hotter than we have."

"What does the thermometer say?" said my uncle.

"Scarcely 15 degrees Centigrade, which is only an increase of nine since our departure."

"Well, and what is your conclusion?"

"According to the most exact observations, the increase of the temperature of the interior of the earth is one degree for every hundred feet. But certain local causes may considerably modify this figure. At Yakoust in Siberia, it has been noted that the heat increases one degree every thirty-six feet. The difference evidently depends on the conductibility of certain rocks. In the neighborhood of an extinct volcano, it has been remarked that the elevation of temperatures was only one degree for every one hundred twenty-five feet. Let us, then, go upon this calculation — which is the most favorable — and calculate."

"Calculate away, my boy."

I pulled out my notebook and pencil. "Nine times one hundred and twenty-five feet make a depth of eleven hundred and twenty-five feet."

"Well," said my uncle, "according to *my* calculations, we are at least ten thousand feet below the level of the sea."

His calculations were perfectly correct. We were already six thousand feet deeper down in the bowels of the earth than anyone had ever been before.

The temperature, which should have been 81° Centigrade, was in this place only 15° (59° Fahrenheit). That was a matter for serious consideration.

The Eastern Tunnel

The next day was Tuesday, the 2nd of July, and at six o'clock in the morning we resumed our journey.

We continued to follow the gallery of lava, a perfect natural pathway. This went on until seventeen minutes past twelve, the precise instant at which we rejoined Hans who, having been somewhat in advance, had suddenly stopped.

"At last," cried my uncle, "we have reached the end of the shaft."

I looked about me. We were in the center of four cross paths — somber and narrow tunnels. The question now arose as to which to take.

My uncle at once made up his mind. He pointed to the eastern tunnel, and we entered its gloomy recesses.

The descent of this obscure and narrow gallery was very gradual and winding. Sometimes we gazed through a succession of arches, very like the aisles of a Gothic cathedral.

Suddenly we would come upon a series of low subterranean tunnels which looked like beaver holes through whose narrow and winding ways we had literally to crawl!

The heat still remained at quite a supportable degree. My uncle's only idea was to go ahead. He walked, he slid, he clambered over piles of fragments, he rolled down heaps of broken lava with an earnestness it was impossible not to admire.

At six o'clock, after a wearisome journey, we had made six miles toward the south, but had not gone more than a mile downwards.

We halted, ate our meal in thoughtful silence, and then retired to sleep. A traveling rug, in which each rolled himself, was all our bedding. Absolute solitude reigned supreme.

We awoke fresh and ready for action. We continued to burrow through the lava tunnel as before. The tunnel, however, instead of going down became absolutely horizontal.

About ten o'clock in the day I was obliged to slacken my pace and finally to come to a halt.

"Well," said the professor, quickly. "What is the matter?"

"I am dreadfully tired," I replied.

"How can that be, when all you have to do is go downwards?"

"I beg your pardon, sir. For some time I have noticed that we are going *upwards*."

"Upwards!" cried my uncle. "How can that be?"

"For the last half hour the slopes have been upward. If we go on in this way we shall find ourselves back in Iceland."

My uncle shook his head. He was not convinced.

I took up my load, and followed Hans, who was now in advance of us. I was anxious not to lose sight of my companions. The very idea of being left behind, lost in that terrible labyrinth, made me shiver.

Besides, if the path was ascending it was hopefully taking us back to the surface of the earth.

About twelve o'clock there was a sudden change in the rocky sides of the gallery. From being coated with shining lava, they became living rock. The sides were sloping walls, which sometimes became quite vertical.

We were now in the period of Silurian

stones, so called because this formation is very common in England in the counties formerly inhabited by the Celtic nation known as Silures.

"I can see clearly now," I cried.

"What is the matter now?" my uncle asked.

"Well," I cried, "do you not see these different layers of calcareous rocks, and the first indication of slate strata?"

"Well, what about it?"

"We have arrived at that period of the world's existence when the first plants and the first animals made their appearance."

"You think so?"

"Yes. Look, examine, and judge for yourself."

I induced the professor to cast the light of his lamp on the sides of the long winding gallery. The professor never spoke a word.

Perhaps it was possible that in his pride my uncle did not like to own that he was wrong in having chosen the eastern tunnel. It was quite evident we had left the region of lava. As we went along, I asked myself if I did not put too great a stress on these peculiar modifications of the earth's crust.

After all, I was very likely to be mistaken. "But if I am right," I thought to myself, "I must certainly find some remains of primitive plants."

I accordingly lost no opportunity of searching, and had not gone more than about a hundred yards, when the evidence I sought for cropped up. It was quite natural that I should expect to find these signs, for during the Silurian period the seas contained no fewer than fifteen hundred different animal and vegetable species. Suddenly I found myself treading on a kind of soft dust, the remains of plants and shells.

Professor Hardwigg, I believe, deliberately closed his eyes to the matter and continued on his way with a firm and unalterable step.

Thinking that he was carrying his obstinancy too far, I could no longer be quiet. I stooped suddenly and picked up an almost perfect shell. I followed my uncle.

"Do you see this?" I said.

"It is the shell of a crustaceous animal of the extinct order of the trilobites," said the professor tranquilly. "Nothing more, I assure you."

"But," I cried, much troubled at his coolness, "do you draw no conclusion from it?"

"Well, what conclusion do you draw?"

"I thought — "

"I know, my boy. You are perfectly right. We have finally abandoned the crust of lava, and the road by which the lava ascended. It is quite possible that I may have been mistaken, but I shall be unable to discover my error until I get to the end of this gallery."

"You are quite right, and I should highly approve of your decision, if we had not to fear the greatest of all dangers."

"And what is that?"

"Want of water."

"Well, my dear Harry, we must put ourselves on rations."

And on he went.

Deeper and Deeper—
the Coal Mine

We were compelled to put ourselves on rations. Our supply would last only three days. In the transition rocks, it was hardly to be expected we would meet with water!

The next day we proceeded through this interminable gallery, arch after arch, tunnel after tunnel, without exchanging a word.

Sometimes there could be no doubt that we were going downwards, but the transitional character of the rocks became more and more marked.

It was a glorious sight to see how the electric light brought out the sparkles in the walls of the calcareous rocks and the old red sandstone. Magnificent specimens of marble projected from the sides of the gallery. Some of these marbles were stamped with the marks of primitive animals.

It was quite evident to me that we were

ascending the scale of animal life with man at the summit. The professor appeared not to take notice of these warnings.

He must have expected one of two things: either that a vertical well was about to open under our feet, and thus allow us to continue our descent, or that some insurmountable obstacle would compel us to stop and go back by the road we had so long traveled. To my horror neither hope was to be realized!

On Friday, after a night when I began to feel the gnawing agony of thirst, we rose and once more followed the ascents and descents of this interminable gallery.

After about ten hours of further progress the reflection of our lamps on the sides of the tunnel dimmed. The marble, the schist, the calcareous rocks, the red sandstone, had disappeared, leaving in their places a dark and gloomy wall. I leaned my left hand against the rock. When I took it away, it was quite black. We had reached the coal strata of the central earth.

"A coal mine!" I cried.

"A coal mine without miners," responded my uncle.

"How can you tell?"

"I can tell," replied my uncle, in a sharp

and dictatorial tone. "I am perfectly certain that this gallery through successive layers of coal was not cut by the hand of man. But the hour for our evening meal has come — let us sup."

Hans occupied himself in preparing food. I could no longer eat. All I cared about were the few drops of water which fell to my share. The guide's gourd, not quite half full, was all that was left for the three of us!

Having finished their meal, my two companions laid themselves down upon their rugs, and fell asleep. I could not sleep. I counted the hours until morning.

The next morning, Saturday, at six o'clock, we started again. Suddenly we came upon a vast excavation.

This mighty natural cavern was about a hundred feet wide by about a hundred and fifty high.

The whole history of the coal period was written on those dark and gloomy walls. The seams of coal were separated by strata of sandstone, a compact clay, which appeared to be crushed down by the weight from above.

At that period of the world which preceded the secondary epoch, the earth was covered by a coating of rich vegetation. A vast cloud of vapor surrounded the earth on all sides, preventing the rays of the sun from ever reaching it.

Climates did not as yet exist and a level heat pervaded the whole surface of the globe; the same heat existing at the north pole as at the equator.

Did it come from the interior of the earth?

In spite of all the learned theories of Professor Hardwigg, a fierce and vehement fire certainly burned within the great globe. Its action was felt even to the very topmost crust of the earth; the plants then in existence, being deprived of the sun, had neither buds, nor flowers, nor odor, but their roots drew a strong vigorous life from the burning earth of early days.

There were few of what may be called trees, only herbaceous plants, immense turfs, and mosses — which in those days could be counted by the tens of thousands.

Coal owes its origin to this exuberant vegetation. The crust of the globe yielded under the seething, boiling mass, which was forever at work beneath it. There was a continual falling-in of the upper crust of the earth.

Then came about the action of natural chemistry. The vegetable mass at first became turf, then underwent the complete process of mineralization.

In this manner, in early days, those vast layers of coal were formed. They must be utterly used up in about three centuries if people do not find some more economic light than gas and some cheaper motive power than steam.

All these reflections came to my mind while I gazed upon these mighty accumulations of coal.

While we journeyed, I forgot the length of the road. The temperature continued to be very much the same. My sense of smell was affected by a very powerful odor. The gallery was filled to overflowing with that dangerous gas the miners call firedamp.

Happily we were able to light our progress by means of the Ruhmkorf apparatus. If we had explored this gallery by torch, a terrible explosion would have put an end to our travels.

By evening, my uncle was scarcely able to conceal his impatience as the road continued horizontally.

The darkness, dense and opaque, made it impossible to make out the length of the gallery.

Suddenly, at six o'clock, we stood in front

of a wall. To the right, to the left, above, below, nowhere was there any passage.

I stood stupefied. The guide simply folded his arms. My uncle was silent.

"Well, well," cried my uncle, at last. "I now know what we are about. We are decidedly not upon the road followed by Saknussemm. All we have to do is to go back. Let us take one night's good rest and before three days are over, I promise you we shall have regained the point where the galleries divided."

"Yes, we may, if our strength lasts that long," I cried.

"And why not?"

"Tomorrow, there will not be a drop of water left. It will be gone."

"And your courage with it," said my uncle, severely.

I turned away. From sheer exhaustion I fell into a heavy but troubled sleep. Dreams of water! I awoke unrefreshed.

I would have bartered a diamond mine for a glass of pure spring water.

The Wrong Road!

Next day we departed at a very early hour. There was no time for delay. It took five days' hard work to get back to the place where the galleries divided.

My uncle bore the sufferings we endured with suppressed anger, Hans with all the resignation of his peaceful character. And I — I confess that I did nothing but complain and despair. I had no heart for this bad fortune.

There was one consolation. Defeat at the outset might upset the whole journey!

As I had expected, our supply of water gave out on our first day's march. Our provision of liquids was reduced to our supply of schiedam. But this horrible liquor burnt the throat, and I could not even bear the sight of it. The temperature was stifling. I was almost paralyzed with fatigue. More than once I was about to fall unconscious to the ground. The whole party then halted, and Hans and my uncle did their best to comfort me. I could plainly see that my uncle too was suffering with extreme fatigue and the awful torture of no water.

At length a time came when I ceased to recollect anything — when all was one awful, hideous, fantastic dream!

At last, on Tuesday, the ninth of the month of July, after crawling on our hands and knees for many hours, we reached the point of junction between the galleries. I lay like a log on the arid lava soil. It was then ten in the morning.

Hans and my uncle, leaning against the wall, tried to nibble away at some pieces of biscuit, while deep groans and sighs escaped my scorched and swollen lips.

Presently, I felt my uncle approach and lift me up tenderly in his arms.

"Poor boy," I heard him say in a tone of deep commiseration.

I was profoundly touched by these words, being by no means accustomed to such signs of tenderness in the professor. His eyes were wet with tears.

I then saw him take the gourd which he wore at his side. To my surprise, he placed it to my lips.

"Drink, my boy," he said.

Was it possible? Was my uncle mad?

"Drink," he said again.

Had I heard right? A mouthful of water cooled my parched lips and throat. One mouthful, but I do believe it brought me back to life.

I thanked my uncle by clasping my hands. My heart was too full to speak.

"Yes," said he, "one mouthful of water, the very last — I saved it for you. I knew that when you reached this crossroad in the earth, you would be half dead."

As little as my thirst was quenched, I had nevertheless partially recovered my strength. The contracted muscles of my throat relaxed. I was able to speak.

"Well," I said, "we know now what we have to do. Our journey is ended. Let us go back to Sneffels."

"Go back," said my uncle, speaking to himself. "Must it be so?"

"Yes," I cried.

For some moments there was silence.

"So, my dear Harry," said the professor, "those few drops of water have not restored courage."

"Courage!" I cried. "You are not discouraged, sir?"

114

"What! Give up just as we are on the verge of success?" he cried. "Never, never shall it be said that Professor Hardwigg retreated."

"Then we must make up our minds to perish," I cried.

"No, Harry my boy, certainly not. Go, leave me. I am very far from desiring your death. Take Hans with you. *I will go on alone.*"

"You ask us to leave you?"

"I have undertaken this dangerous and perilous adventure. I will carry it through to the end or I will never return to the surface of the earth. Go, Harry! Once more I say to you — go!"

My uncle was terribly excited. His voice became menacing. I did not wish to abandon him at the bottom of that abyss, but the instinct for preservation told me to fly.

Meanwhile Hans, who was looking on, appeared to be unconcerned and yet he perfectly well knew what was going on between us.

It was really a question of life and death for us all, but Hans waited, quite ready to obey the signal to go back or into the interior of the earth. I wished with all my heart and soul that I could make him understand my words.

I caught his hand in mine. He never moved a muscle. I indicated to him the road to the top of the crater. The Icelander gently shook his head and pointed to my uncle.

"Master," he said.

The word is Icelandic as well as English.

"The master!" I cried, beside myself with fury. *"Madman!* No — I tell you he is not the master of our lives. We must fly, we must drag him with us! Do you hear me? Do you understand me?"

I held Hans by the arm. I tried to make him rise from his seat. My uncle now intervened.

"My good Harry, be calm," he said. "You will get nowhere with my devoted follower. Listen therefore to what I have to say."

I looked my uncle full in the face.

"This wretched want of water," he said, "is the sole obstacle to the success of my project. It is true we found not one liquid molecule. It is quite possible that we may be more fortunate in the western tunnel." I shook my head, incredulous.

"Listen to me to the end," said the professor. "While you lay yonder, I went reconnoitering to this other gallery. It goes directly downwards into the earth, and in a few hours will take us to the old granite formation. In this we shall undoubtedly find springs. The nature of the rock makes this a mathematical certainty.

"I have a serious proposition to make to you. When Christopher Columbus asked his men for three more days to discover the land of promise, his men, ill, terrified, and hopeless, gave him three days — and the New World was discovered. Now I, the Christopher Columbus of this subterranean region, ask of you only one more day. If, when that time is expired, I have not found the water of which we are in search, I swear to you I will give up my mighty enterprise and return to the earth's surface."

Despite my despair, I knew how much it cost my uncle to make this proposition. What could I do but yield?

"Well," I cried, "let it be as you wish. But unless we discover water, our hours are numbered. Let us lose no time, but go ahead."

The Western Gallery— a New Route

H ans took up his post in front, as usual. We had not gone more than a hundred yards when the professor carefully examined the walls.

"This is the primitive formation. We are on the right road."

When the whole earth cooled, in the first hours of the world's morning, the shrinking of the earth produced ruptures, crevasses, and fissures in the crust. The passage we were in was a fissure of this kind.

As we descended, successions of layers composing the primitive soil appeared. This primitive soil is the base of the mineral crust and it is composed of three different strata, or layers, all resting on the immovable rock known as granite.

No mineralogists had ever found themselves placed in such a marvelous position. We were about to see with our own eyes, to touch with our own hands, the earth's internal structure.

Remember that I am writing this *after* the journey.

Across the streak of the rocks, colored by beautiful green tints, wound metallic threads of copper and manganese, with traces of platinum and gold.

The light of our Ruhmkorf coil sent jets of fire in every direction. I could fancy myself traveling through a huge hollow diamond, the rays of which produced myriads of extraordinary effects.

Toward six o'clock, this festival of light began to decrease, and soon almost ceased. The sides of the gallery assumed a crystallized tint with a somber hue. White mica began to mingle more freely with feldspar and quartz, to form the true rock — the stone that supports, without being crushed, the four stories of the earth's soil.

We were walled in an immense prison of granite!

It was now eight o'clock, and still there was no sign of water. My suffering was horrible. My uncle, now in the lead, could not stop. My ear was keenly alert to catch the sound of a spring. But no sound of falling water fell upon my listening ear.

At last the time came when my limbs refused to carry me. I felt a deadly faintness come over me. My eyes could not see, my knees shook. I gave one despairing cry — and fell!

"Help, help, I am dying!"

My uncle turned and slowly retraced his steps. He looked at me with folded arms, and then allowed one sentence to escape from his lips.

"All is over."

The last thing I saw was a face fearfully distorted with pain and sorrow, then my eyes closed.

When I again opened my eyes, I saw my companions lying near me, wrapped in their huge traveling rugs. Were they asleep or dead? For myself, sleep was wholly out of the question. My fainting fit over, I was wakeful as the lark. I suffered too much to sleep, for I thought I was dying. The last words spoken by my uncle seemed to be buzzing in my ears — *all is over!* Probably he was right. In my state of prostration it was madness to think of ever again seeing the light of day.

Above me was mile upon mile of the earth's crust. Hour upon hour passed away. A terrible silence reigned around us — a silence of the tomb. Nothing could make itself heard through these gigantic walls of granite.

Presently something aroused me. It was a slight but peculiar noise. I observed that the tunnel was becoming dark. Gazing through the dim light I thought I saw the Icelander taking his departure, lamp in hand.

Why had he acted thus? Did Hans mean to abandon us? My uncle lay fast asleep — or dead. I tried to cry out and arouse him.

But after the first few moments of terror, I was ashamed of my suspicions against a man who hitherto had behaved so admirably. Moreover, instead of ascending the gallery, he was going deeper down into the gulf.

This reasoning calmed me a little, and I began to hope!

Hans would certainly not have arisen from his sleep without some serious and grave motive. Was he bent on the voyage of discovery? Had he at last heard that sweet murmur for which we were all so anxious?

Water, Where Is It?
A Bitter Disappointment

During a long, weary hour there crossed my delirious brain all sorts of reasons as to what could have aroused our faithful guide.

Presently an uncertain light came in view far down the sloping tunnel. At length Hans himself appeared. He approached my uncle, placed his hand on his shoulder, and gently awakened him. My uncle instantly rose.

"Well!" exclaimed the professor.

"Vatten," said the hunter.

I did not know a single word of the Danish language, and yet I understood what the guide had said.

"Water, water!" I cried, frantically.

"Water!" murmured my uncle. *"Hvar?"* ("Where?")

"Nedat." ("Below.")

"Where? Below!" I understood every word. I caught Hans by the hand.

We lost no time descending into the tunnel. An hour later we had advanced a thousand yards and descended two thousand feet.

At this moment I heard a kind of dull and sullen roar along the floors of the granite rock — like that of a distant waterfall.

"Hans was right," my uncle exclaimed enthusiastically. "That dull roar is a torrent of water."

"A torrent," I cried, delighted at the welcome words.

"There's not the slightest doubt about it," he repled. "A subterranean river is flowing beside us."

I made no reply but hastened on, once more animated by hope. I began to lose the deep fatigue which had overpowered me. The very sound of this glorious murmuring water already refreshed me. The torrent ran distinctly along the left wall, roaring, rushing, spluttering, and still falling.

Several times I passed my hand across the rock, hoping to find some trace of humidity. Alas! in vain.

Again a half hour passed in the same weary toil. Again we advanced.

It now became evident that Hans had only

heard the living spring through the rock. He had not seen the precious liquid or quenched his thirst.

Moreover, we soon made the disastrous discovery that we were moving away from the torrent. We turned back. Hans halted at the precise spot where the sound of the torrent appeared nearest.

We could bear the suspense and suffering no longer, and seated ourselves against the wall. I could hear the water seething not two feet away. But behind a solid wall of granite!

Hans looked at me, and for once I thought I saw a smile on his imperturbable face.

He rose and took up the lamp. I could not help following. He moved slowly along the solid granite wall. Presently he halted and placed his ear against the dry stone, listening carefully. He was searching for the exact spot where the torrent's roar was most plainly heard. This point he soon found on the left side of the gallery, about three feet above the level of the tunnel floor.

I scarcely dared believe what our guide was about to do when I saw him raise the heavy crowbar and begin to dig at the rock.

"Saved," I cried.

"Yes," cried my uncle, even more excited and delighted than myself. "Hans is quite right. We should never have thought of such an idea."

And nobody else, I think, would have dared to. Nothing could be more dangerous than to begin to work with pickaxes in that place. Supposing the torrent once having gained an inch were to come pouring through the broken rock!

These dangers were only too real. But at that moment no fear was capable of stopping us; our thirst was too intense.

Hans went quietly to work. At the end of what appeared an age, he had made a hole with the crowbar about two feet into the solid rock. He had been at work exactly an hour. It seemed a dozen. I was growing wild with impatience. My uncle was considering using more violent measures when a loud and welcome noise was heard. Then a jet of water burst through the wall with such force that it hit the opposite side!

Hans, who was almost knocked down by the force of the water, could barely hold back a cry of pain. I understood why immediately and myself gave a frantic cry. The water was scalding hot!

"Boiling," I cried, in bitter disappointment.

"Well, never mind," said my uncle. "It will soon get cool."

The tunnel began to fill with clouds of

vapor, while a small stream ran away into the interior of the earth. In a short time we had scooped up some water and it cooled sufficiently to drink. We swallowed it in huge mouthfuls.

Oh, what rich and incomparable luxury. It brought back life which, but for it, must surely have faded away. I drank greedily, almost without tasting it.

Then I made a discovery.

"Why, it is ferruginous water!"

"Most excellent for the stomach," replied my uncle, "highly mineralized. Here is a journey worth twenty to a spa."

"It's very good," I replied.

"I should think so. What do you say, nephew, to naming the stream after Hans?"

"Good," I said. And the name of "Hansbach" was at once agreed upon.

Unimpressed, Hans took a very small amount of water, then seated himself in a corner with his usual gravity.

"Now," I said, "we cannot let this water run to waste."

"It is all right," replied my uncle. "The source from which this river rises is inexhaustible."

"Never mind," I continued. "Let us fill our goatskin and gourds, and then try to stop up the opening."

After some hesitation, Hans attempted to follow my advice. But all he did was to scald his hands. The pressure was too great.

"It is evident," I remarked, "from the great pressure of the jet that these springs rise at a very great height above us."

"That must be so," replied my uncle. "The pressure must be something enormous. But a new idea has just struck me. Why try to close this aperture? When the containers are empty, we are not at all sure that we shall be able to fill them."

"That is probable," I said.

"Well, then, let this water run. It will serve to guide, and to refresh us."

"A good idea," I cried in reply. "And with this rivulet as a companion, there is no further reason why we should not succeed in our marvelous project."

"Ah, my boy," said the professor, laughing, "you are coming around after all."

"More than that, I am now confident of ultimate success."

"One moment, nephew mine. Let us begin by taking some hours of rest."

Soon we had all fallen into a deep sleep.

Under the Ocean

By the next day we had nearly forgotten our sufferings. The running stream, which flowed at my feet, was the reason.

I felt ready to go anywhere my uncle chose to lead. Indeed, had the proposition now been made to go back to the summit of Mount Sneffels, I should have declined the offer indignantly.

We resumed our march into the interior of the earth on Thursday at eight o'clock in the morning. The great granite tunnel going round by sinuous and winding ways had the appearance of a labyrinth. Its direction, however, was in general toward the southwest. My uncle consulted his compass repeatedly.

The gallery began to wind downward with about two inches of fall in every furlong. The murmuring stream flowed quietly at our feet, like some familiar spirit guiding us through the earth.

My uncle began to complain of the horizontal character of the road. But as long as our road led toward the center there was no reason to complain. From time to time, however, the slope was much greater, and we began to dip downward in earnest.

On Friday evening, the twelfth of July, according to our estimation we were thirty leagues to the southwest of Reykjavik and about two leagues and a half deep. We now received a rather startling surprise.

Under our feet there opened a horrible well. My uncle was delighted when he saw how steep and sharp was the descent.

"Ah, ah!" he cried, in rapturous delight. "This will take us a long way. Look at the projections of the rock. Hah!" he exclaimed, "it's a fearful staircase!"

Hans, however, took care to handle the ropes so as to prevent any accidents. Our descent then began.

This well was a kind of narrow opening, known as a fissure, in the massive granite. We were descending a spiral, something like those winding staircases in use in modern houses.

We were often compelled to rest our legs.

Our calves ached. We then seated ourselves on some projecting rock with our legs hanging over. The Hansbach had become a narrow cascade but it was still sufficient for our wants.

During the whole of two days, the thirteenth and fourteenth of July, we followed the extraordinary spiral staircase of the fissure, penetrating two leagues farther into the crust of the earth, which placed us five leagues below the level of the sea. On the fifteenth, at twelve noon, the fissure suddenly assumed a much more gentle slope.

The road now became comparatively easy, and at the same time, dreadfully monotonous.

At length, on Wednesday, the seventeenth, we were actually seven leagues (twenty-one miles) below the surface of the earth, and fifty leagues distant from the mountain of Sneffels. We were very tired, but our health was most satisfactory. Our box of medicines had not even been opened.

Every hour my uncle carefully noted the readings of the compass, the manometer, and the thermometer. All of which he later published in his elaborate philosophical and scientific account of our remarkable voyage. When he informed me that we were fifty leagues in a horizontal direction from our starting point, I could not suppress a loud exclamation.

"What is the matter now?" asked my uncle.

"If your calculations are correct, we are no longer under Iceland," I replied, pulling out the map. "You see," I said, after careful measurement, "we are -far beyond Cape Portland. Those fifty leagues to the southwest have taken us into the open sea."

"Under the open sea," cried my uncle, rubbing his hands with a delighted air.

"Yes," I cried. "No doubt the old ocean flows over our heads."

"Do you know, my dear boy, that in the neighborhood of Newcastle there are coal mines which have been worked far out under the sea?"

Now my uncle regarded this as a very natural thing, but to me the idea was not pleasant. The whole question rested on the solidity of the granite roof above us.

Three days later, on July twentieth, a Saturday, we reached a kind of vast grotto. My uncle paid Hans his usual rix-dollars, and it was decided that the next day should be a day of rest.

Sunday Below Ground

I awoke on Sunday morning without any sense of the hurry and bustle attendant on departure. After breakfast the professor devoted some hours to putting his notes in order.

"In the first place," he said, "I want to verify our exact position. I wish to be able, on our return, to make a map of our journey — a kind of vertical section of the globe as a profile of the expedition."

"But can you make your observations with certainty and precision?"

"I can. I have made notes of all angles and slopes. Take the compass and examine how she points."

I looked at the instrument. "East one quarter southeast."

"Very good." The professor made some

rapid calculations. We have journeyed two hundred and fifty miles from the point of our departure."

"Then the Atlantic *is* over our heads?"

"Certainly."

"We are two hundred and fifty miles to the southeast of Sneffels, and I think we have gone sixteen leagues in a downward direction."

"Sixteen leagues — fifty miles!" I cried.

"I am sure of it."

"But that is the extreme limit allowed by science for the thickness of the earth's crust."

"I do not deny that," was his quiet answer.

"And at this point in our journey, according to all known laws on the increase of heat, the temperature should be about 1500° Centigrade." (2732° F.)

"It should be, you say, my boy."

"In which case this granite would not exist, but be in a state of fusion."

"But you can see, my boy, that it is not so. Facts are very stubborn things, overruling all theories."

"I am forced to yield, but I am surprised."

"What heat *does* the thermometer indicate?" continued the professor.

"Centigrade degrees 27.6." (81.6° F.)

"So that science is wrong by over fourteen hundred degrees. The proportional increase in temperature is an exploded theory. Humphrey Davy is right, and I have acted wisely to believe in him."

"Well, sir," I said, "I take for granted that all your calculations are correct, but allow me to draw from them a rigorous conclusion."

"Go on, my boy, have your say," cried my uncle good-humoredly.

"At the place where we now are, the terrestrial depth is thought to be about fifteen hundred and eighty-three leagues. Now out of a voyage of, say, sixteen hundred leagues, we have completed sixteen and we have been twenty days about it. Now sixteen is the hundredth part of our contemplated expedition. If we go on in this way we shall be five years and a half going down."

The professor folded his arms, listened, but did not speak.

"Now added to that, our vertical descent of sixteen leagues has cost us a horizontal of eighty-five. We shall have to go about eight thousand leagues to the southeast and we must therefore come out somewhere on the circumference long before we can hope to reach the center."

"Bother your calculations," cried my uncle, in one of his old rages. "On what basis do they rest? How do you know that this passage does not take us direct to the end we require? Moreover, I have a precedent. What I have undertaken to do, another has done, and he succeeded. Why should I not be equally successful?"

"I hope you will. But still, may I be allowed to — "

"You are allowed to hold your tongue," cried Professor Hardwigg, "when you talk so unreasonably as this."

I saw at once that the "old professor" was still alive in my uncle. I dropped the subject.

"Now, then," he ordered. "Consult the manometer. What does that indicate?"

"A considerable amount of pressure."

"Very good. You see, then, that by descending slowly and by gradually accustoming ourselves to the density of this lower atmosphere, we shall not suffer."

"Well, I suppose not, except there may be a certain amount of pain in the ears."

"That, my dear boy, is nothing. You will easily get rid of that by bringing the exterior air into your lungs."

"Agreed," said I, determined not to contradict my uncle. "Have you noticed how wonderfully sound increases in this dense atmosphere?"

"Of course I have. A journey into the interior of the earth would be an excellent cure for deafness."

"But then, Uncle," I ventured mildly, "this density will continue to increase."

Yes, according to a law which is scarcely defined. It is true that the intensity of weight will diminish in proportion to the depth to which we go. You know very well that on the surface of the earth the intensity is most powerfully felt. While in the center of the earth bodies cease to have any weight at all." [1]

It was evident to *me* that the air, under a pressure which might be multiplied by thousands of atmospheres, would end by becoming perfectly solid. Then, if our bodies resisted the pressure, we should have to stop in spite of all the reasoning in the world.

But I thought it best not to push this argument. My uncle would simply have quoted the example of Saknussemm. And there was one simple answer to be made to that:

In the sixteenth century, neither the barometer nor the manometer had been invent-

[1] This was a theory in Jules Verne's day.

ed. How, then, could Saknussemm have been able to discover when he did reach the center of the earth?

This objection I kept to myself and awaited the course of events — little aware of how adventurous the incidents of our remarkable journey were yet to be.

For the rest of this day of rest, I made it a point to agree with the professor in everything. I envied the perfect indifference of Hans, who went blindly onwards wherever destiny chose to lead him.

Alone

It must be confessed, things so far had gone on well and it was possible that we might ultimately reach the end of our journey. Then what glory would be ours!

For several days after our memorable halt, the slopes became more rapid. Some were almost vertical, so that we were forever going down into the solid interior mass. During some days, we actually descended two leagues toward the center of the earth. The descents were sufficiently perilous, and we learned fully to appreciate the marvelous coolness of our guide. Without Hans we should have been wholly lost.

His silence seemed to increase every day. I think that we began to be influenced by this peculiar trait in his character.

During the three weeks that followed our

last interesting conversation, there occurred nothing worthy of being recorded.

But the next event to be related is terrible indeed. Its very memory, even now, makes my soul shudder and my blood run cold.

It was on the seventh of August. Our successive descents had taken us quite thirty leagues into the interior of the earth. Above us there were thirty leagues — nearly a hundred miles — of rocks and oceans and continents and towns, to say nothing of living inhabitants. We were about two hundred leagues southeast of Iceland.

On that memorable day, the tunnel had begun to assume an almost horizontal course.

I was, on this occasion, walking in front. My uncle had charge of one of the Ruhmkorf coils. I had possession of the other. By means of its light I was busy examining the different layers of granite. I was completely absorbed in my work.

Suddenly halting and turning around, I found that I was alone!

"Well," thought I to myself, "I have been walking too fast, or else Hans and my uncle have stopped to rest. The best thing I can do is to go back and find them. Luckily, there is very little ascent to tire me."

I retraced my steps, walking for at least

a quarter of an hour. Rather uneasy, I paused and looked eagerly around. I called aloud. No reply. My voice was lost amid the myriad echoes it aroused!

I began for the first time to feel seriously uneasy. A cold shiver shook my whole body, and perspiration, chill and terrible, burst upon my skin.

"I must be calm," I said, speaking aloud. "There can be no doubt that I shall find my companions. There cannot be two roads. It is certain that I was considerably ahead. All I have to do is to go back."

Having come to this determination, I continued along the tunnel for another half hour, unable to decide if I had ever seen certain landmarks before. Every now and then I listened to hear if anyone was calling me. Only the echoes of my own footsteps could be heard.

At last I stopped. I could scarcely realize the fact of my isolation. I was quite willing to believe that I had made a mistake, but not that I was lost. If I had made a mistake, I might find my way. If lost — I shuddered to think of it.

"Come," I said to myself, "since there is only one road and they must come by it, we shall meet. All I have to do is continue upwards. Perhaps not seeing me and forgetting I was ahead, they have gone back in search of me. Even in this case, if I make haste, I shall catch up to them. There can be no doubt."

But as I spoke these last words aloud, I was by no means convinced of the fact.

Then another dread doubt fell upon my soul. Was I ahead? Of course I was. Hans was following behind. I recollected his having stopped for a moment to strap his baggage on his shoulder. I now perfectly remembered this trifling detail. It was just at that very moment that I determined to continue my route.

Reasoning as calmly as was possible, I thought, "There is another sure means of not losing my way, our faithful river."

This course of reasoning roused my drooping spirits and I resolved to resume my journey without further delay. No time was to be lost.

Having come to this decision, I stopped to plunge my hands and forehead in the pleasant water of the Hansbach.

Conceive my horror and stupefaction! I was treading a hard, dusty, shingly road of granite. The stream had disappeared!

Lost!

No words in any human language can describe my utter despair. I was literally buried alive, with no expectation but to die in all the slow, horrible torture of hunger and thirst.

I crawled about, feeling the dry and arid rock. How had I lost the course of the stream? Now I began to understand the strange silence which prevailed when I tried to listen for any sound from my companions.

It was now quite evident that I had unconsciously entered a different gallery. To what unknown depths had my companions gone? Where was I?

How to get back! Clue or landmark, there was absolutely none! My feet left no signs on the granite and shingle. My brain throbbed as I tried to solve this terrible problem. My situation had finally to be summed up in three awful words:

Lost! Lost! LOST!!!

Lost at a depth which seemed to me immeasurable.

I tried to bring my thoughts back to the things of the world so long forgotten: Hamburg, the house on the Konigstrasse, my dear cousin Gretchen. There they were before me, but how unreal!

Then I saw all the incidents of our journey pass before me. I said to myself that if I retained the most shadowy outline of a hope, it must surely be a sign of approaching delirium. Who could help me to find my road, and regain my companions?

It was folly and madness to entertain even a shadow of hope!

"Oh, Uncle!" was my despairing cry.

At last I began to resign myself to the fact that no further aid was to be expected from man. Knowing that I was powerless to do anything for my own salvation, I prayed earnestly and sincerely.

This renewal of my youthful faith brought about a great calm, and I was able to concentrate all my strength and intelligence on the terrible realities of my situation.

I had three days' provisions. Moreover, my water bottle was quite full. Nevertheless, it was impossible to remain alone. I must try to find my companions at any price. Doubtless I was right to retrace my steps in an upward direction.

By doing this with care and coolness, I must reach the point where I had turned away from the rippling stream. Once at this spot, once the river was at my feet, I could regain the awful crater of Mount Sneffels.

After a slight meal and a drink of water, I rose refreshed. Leaning heavily on my pole, I began the ascent of the gallery. The slope was very rapid, but I advanced hopefully and carefully.

During one whole hour nothing happened to check my progress. As I advanced I tried to recall the shape of the tunnel to persuade myself that I had followed this winding route before. But no one particular sign could I remember. I was soon forced to admit that this gallery would never take me back to the point at which I had separated from my companions. It was absolutely without an cpening — a mere blind alley in the earth.

The moment at length came when, facing the solid rock, I knew my fate. The courage which had sustained me drooped before the sight of this pitiless granite rock! All that remained for me was to lie down and die. To lie down and die the most cruel and horrible of deaths!

In the midst of all this anguish and despair, a new horror befell me. My lamp, by falling down, had got out of order. I had no means of repairing it. Its light was already becoming paler and paler, and would soon expire.

With a strange sense of resignation and despair, I watched a procession of shadows flash along the granite wall. I scarcely dared to lower my eyelids, fearing to lose the last spark of this fugitive light. Every instant it seemed to me that it was about to vanish and to leave me forever — in utter darkness!

At last, one final trembling flame remained in the lamp. I followed it with all my power of vision. I gasped for breath. I concentrated upon it all the power of my soul, as if this was the last light I was ever destined to see.

A wild cry escaped my lips. On earth light is never completely extinguished. It permeates everywhere, and whatever little may remain, the retina of the eye will succeed in finding it. In this place nothing — not the faintest ray of light.

I was now wholly lost. I knew not what I did. I began to run, always screaming, roaring, howling, falling and picking myself up all covered with blood.

Where was I going? It was impossible to say. I was perfectly ignorant of the matter.

After a long time, having utterly exhausted my strength, I fell along the side of the tunnel and lost all consciousness of existence!

The Whispering Gallery

When I at last came back to a sense of life, my face was wet; but wet as I soon knew with tears. How long my state of insensibility had lasted, it is impossible for me to say. Never since the creation of the world had such a solitude as mine existed. I was completely abandoned.

After my fall I lost much blood. My first sensation was perhaps a natural one. Why was I not dead? I tried to stop thinking. As far as I was able, I drove away all ideas. Utterly overcome by pain and grief, I crouched against the granite wall.

I began to feel the fainting coming on again when a violent uproar reached my ears. It bore some resemblance to the prolonged rumbling of thunder, and I could clearly distinguish voices, lost one after the other in the distant depths of the gulf.

I listened with deep attention. I was extremely anxious to hear if this strange and inexplicable sound was likely to be repeated! I waited in painful expectation. Deep and solemn silence reigned in the tunnel. So still that I could hear the beating of my own heart! I waited, with a strange kind of hopefulness.

Suddenly my ears appeared to catch the faintest echo of a sound. I thought that I heard vague, incoherent, and distant voices. I quivered all over with excitement and hope!

"It must be hallucination," I cried. "It cannot be! It is not true!"

But no! I really did convince myself that what I heard was the sound of human voices. To make out any meaning was beyond my power. I was too weak even to hear distinctly. Still someone was speaking. Of that I was quite certain.

There was a moment of fear, a dread that it might be my own words brought back to me by a distant echo. Perhaps without knowing it, I might have been speaking aloud. I resolutely closed my lips and once more placed my ear to the huge granite wall.

Yes, for certain. It was the sound of human voices.

I dragged myself along the side of the cavern until I reached a point where I could hear more distinctly.

At last, I made out the word *forlorad,* repeated several times in a tone of great anguish and sorrow.

What could this word mean, and who was speaking? It must be either my uncle or Hans! If I could hear them, they must surely be able to hear me.

"Help!" I cried, at the top of my voice.

"Help, I am dying!"

I then listened with scarcely a breath for the slightest sound in the darkness — a cry, a sigh, a question! But silence reigned. No answer came! A whole flood of ideas flashed through my mind. I began to fear that my voice, weakened by sickness and suffering, could not reach my companions who were in search of me.

"It must be them," I cried. "What other men can possibly be buried a hundred miles below the level of the earth?"

I began to listen again with the most breathless attention. As I moved along the side of the tunnel I found a point where the voices appeared to attain their maximum intensity. The word *forlorad* again reached my ear. Then came that rolling noise like thunder.

"I begin to understand," I said to myself. "It is not through the solid mass that the sound reaches my ears. It must come along the gallery itself. The place I am in must possess some peculiar acoustic properties of its own."

Again I listened, and, yes, this time I heard my name distinctly pronounced — cast, as it were, into space.

It was my uncle speaking. He was talking with Hans.

Then I understood. In order to make myself heard, I must speak along the side of the gallery, which would carry the sound of my voice, just as the wire carries electric fluid from point to point.

There was no time to lose. If my companions were to move a few feet from where they stood, the acoustic effect might be gone — my whispering gallery would be destroyed. I turned toward the wall and said as clearly and distinctly as I could:

"Uncle Hardwigg."

I then awaited a reply.

Several seconds elapsed, which to my ex-

cited imagination appeared ages, before
these words reached my eager ears:

"Harry, my boy! Is that you?"

There was a short delay between question
and answer.

"Yes — yes."

"Where are you?"

"Lost!"

"And your lamp?"

"Out."

"But the stream?"

"Is gone."

"Keep your courage, Harry. We will do our
best."

"One moment, Uncle," I cried. "I no longer have the strength to answer your questions. But — for heaven's sake — do — continue — to speak — to me!"

Absolute silent, I felt, would be annihila-
tion.

"Keep up your courage," said my uncle.
"As you are so weak, do not speak. We have
been searching for you in all directions. My
dear boy, I had begun to give up all hope;
you can never know my sorrow and regret.
It may be a long time before we actually
meet. We are conversing by means of some
extraordinary acoustic arrangement of the
labyrinth. But do not despair, my dear boy.

It is something gained even to hear each other."

While he was speaking, my brain was at work. A certain undefined hope, vague and shapeless as yet, made my heart beat wildly. It was absolutely necessary for me to know one thing. Therefore, I leaned my head against the wall and spoke again.

"Uncle."

"My boy," was his ready answer.

"It is of the utmost importance that we know how far we are apart."

"That is not difficult."

"You have your chronometer at hand?" I asked.

"Certainly."

"Well, take it into your hand. Pronounce my name, noting exactly the second at which you speak. I will reply as soon as I hear your words — and you will then note exactly the moment at which my reply reaches you."

"Very good. Between my question and your answer will be the time occupied by my voice in reaching you."

"That is exactly what I mean, Uncle," was my eager reply.

"Are you ready?"

"Yes."

"Well, make ready. I am about to pronounce your name," said the professor.

I put my ear to the side of the gallery, and as soon as the word Harry reached my ear, I placed my lips to the wall and repeated the name.

"Forty seconds," said my uncle. "Forty seconds have elapsed between the two words. The sound, therefore, takes twenty seconds to reach you. Now, allowing one thousand twenty feet for every second, we have twenty thousand four hundred feet — a league and a half plus one eighth."

These words fell on my ear like a death knell.

"A league and a half," I cried in a despairing voice.

"It shall be got over, my boy," cried my uncle, in a cheery tone. "Depend on us."

"But do you know whether I must ascend or descend?" I asked.

"You have to descend. We have reached a vast open space, a kind of crossroad from which galleries diverge in every direction. The gallery in which you are now lying must lead to this place. Rouse yourself. Have courage and continue your route. Walk, if you can. If not, drag yourself along — slide, if nothing else is possible. The slope must be rather steep, and you will find strong arms to receive you at the end of your journey. Make a start, like a good fellow."

These words served to rouse some courage in my sinking frame.

"Farewell for the present, Uncle. Farewell, until we meet again."

"Adieu, Harry — until we say welcome." Such were the last words to reach my anxious ears before I started my weary and almost hopeless journey.

This surprising conversation took place through the vast mass of the earth's labyrinth, the speakers being about five miles apart.

This astounding acoustic mystery is easily explained by simple natural laws: It arose from the conductibility of the rock. I reasoned that if my uncle and I could communicate at so great a distance, then no serious obstacle could exist between us. All I had to do was move in the direction from which the sound had reached me and I must reach him if my strength did not fail.

I rose to my feet. I found that I could not walk, that I must drag myself along. The slope, as I expected, fell off very rapidly, and I allowed myself to slip down.

Soon the pitch of the descent began to assume frightful proportions. I clutched at the sides. I grasped at projecting rocks. I threw myself backwards.

All in vain. I was so weak. I could do nothing to save myself.

Suddenly earth failed me.

I was launched into a dark and gloomy void, a perfect well. My head bounded against a pointed rock, and I lost all knowledge of existence. As far as I was concerned, death had claimed me for his own.

A Rapid Recovery

When I returned to consciousness, I found myself lying on some thick and soft coverlets. My uncle was watching — a grave expression on his face, tears in his eyes. When I sighed he took hold of my hand. When he saw my eyes open and fix themselves upon his, he uttered a loud cry of joy.

"He lives! He lives!"

"Yes, my good uncle!" I whispered.

"My dear boy! You are saved!"

I was deeply touched by the tone in which these words were uttered, and even more by the kindly care which accompanied them. The professor was one of those men who must be severely tried in order to show any display of affection. At this moment Hans joined us. His eyes beamed with lively satisfaction.

"*Good-dag*," he said.

"Good-day, Hans," I replied. "Uncle, tell me where we are. I have lost all idea of our position, as of everything else."

"Tomorrow, Harry, tomorrow," he replied. "Today you are far too weak. Your head is covered with bandages and poultices that must not be touched. Sleep, my boy, and tomorrow you will know all."

"But," I cried, "let me know what time it is. What day it is."

"It is now eleven o'clock at night, Sunday, the eleventh of August. And I will not answer any more questions until the twelfth."

I was very weak, and my eyes soon closed. I realized that my perilous adventure had lasted four days!

On awakening next day, I looked around me. My sleeping place, made of all our traveling bedding, was in a charming grotto. It was adorned with magnificent stalagmites, and the floor was of soft and silvery sand.

No torch, no lamp was lighted and yet certain unexplained beams of light penetrated into the beautiful grotto.

I heard a vague and indefinite murmur, like the ebb and flow of waves upon a beach, and sometimes I actually believed I could hear the sighing of the wind.

157

I began to think that I must be dreaming. Had my brain been affected by my fall? After some reflection, I came to the conclusion that I could not be mistaken. Surely eyes and ears could not both deceive me.

"It is a ray of daylight," I said to myself, "which has penetrated through some mighty fissure in the rocks. But what is the meaning of this murmur of waves, this unmistakable moaning of the sea? I can hear, too, the whistling of the wind. Has my uncle carried me back to the surface of the earth! Has he, on my account, given up his expedition, or has it in some strange manner come to an end?"

I was puzzling over these and other questions when the professor joined me.

"Good-day, Harry," he cried, joyously. "I fancy you are quite well."

"I am very much better," I replied, sitting up.

"I thought you would be, as you slept soundly. Hans and I have each watched over you and every hour we have seen improvement."

"You must be right, Uncle," was my reply, "for I am really hungry."

"You shall eat, my boy, you shall eat."

While he was speaking, my uncle was placing before me several articles of food, which I devoured. As soon as the first hunger was appeased, I overwhelmed him with questions.

I learned that my fall had brought me to the bottom of an almost perpendicular gallery. As I came down, amidst a perfect shower of stones, I was cast headlong into my uncle's arms, insensible and covered with blood.

"It is a miracle," was the professor's final remark, "that you were not killed a thousand times over. Let us take care not to separate again."

These last words fell with a sort of chill upon my heart. The journey, then, was not over. I looked at my uncle in astonishment. After an instant he said:

"What is the matter, Harry?"

"I want to ask you a very serious question. You say that I am all right in health?"

"Certainly you are."

"And all my limbs are sound?" I asked.

"Most undoubtedly."

"But what about my head?" was my next anxious question.

"Well, except for one or two contusions, your head, is exactly where it ought to be — on your shoulders," said my uncle, laughing.

"Well, my own opinion is that my head is not exactly right. In fact, I believe I am slightly delirious."

"What makes you think so?"

"Have we returned to the surface of the earth?"

"Certainly not."

"Then truly I must be mad, for I think I see the light of day and hear the whistling of the wind. And can I not distinguish the wash of a great sea?"

"Is that all that makes you uneasy?" asked my uncle, with a smile.

"Can you explain?"

"I will not make any attempt to explain. You shall see and judge for yourself. Geological science is as yet in its infancy, and we are privileged to enlighten the world."

"Let me see then," I cried, eagerly.

"Wait a moment, my dear Harry," he responded. "You must be careful after your illness before going into the open air."

"The open air?"

"Yes, my boy. The wind is rather violent. Have a little patience. A relapse would be inconvenient. We have no time to lose, as our approaching sea voyage may be of long duration."

"Sea voyage?" I cried, more bewildered than ever.

"Yes. You take another day's rest, and we shall be ready to go on board by tomorrow," replied my uncle, with a peculiar smile.

Go on board! The words utterly astonished me.

Go on board — what and how? Had we come upon a river, a lake? Had we discovered some inland sea? Was a vessel lying at anchor in some part of the interior of the earth?

My curiosity was worked up to the very highest pitch. When my uncle discovered that the satisfaction of my wishes could alone restore me to a calm state of mine, he gave in.

I dressed myself rapidly, and then wrapping myself in one of the coverlets, I rushed out of the grotto.

The Central Sea

My eyes were wholly unused to the sudden brightness, and I was compelled to close them. When I was able to reopen them, I stood still, more stupefied than astonished. My imagination could never have conjured up such a scene!

"The sea — the sea," I cried.

"Yes," replied my uncle. "The Central Sea. No future navigator will deny that I discovered it, and hence have the right to give it a name."

A vast, limitless expanse of water, the end of a lake if not an ocean, spread before us. The shore consisted of beautiful soft golden sand, mixed with small shells. The waves broke incessantly, with a peculiarly sonorous murmur. A light foam flew off the water, and many a dash of spray was blown into my

face. On all sides were capes and promonto-
ries and enormous cliffs. The mighty
superstructure of rock rose above to an
inconceivable height.

It was in reality an ocean, only horribly
wild, cold, and savage.

One thing startled and puzzled me greatly. The landscape before me was lit up, but
had none of the dazzling brilliance of the
sun, the pale illumination of the moon, or the
brightness of the stars. The illuminating
power in this subterraneous region was evidently electric. Its trembling and flickering
character, its clear dry whiteness was something akin to the aurora borealis, only that
it was constant and able to light up the
whole of the ocean cavern.

There were heavy, dense clouds rolling
along that mighty vault, partially concealing
the roof. Electric currents produced astonishing play of light and shade in the distance, especially around the heavier clouds.
Deep shadows were cast beneath and then
suddenly, between two clouds, there would
come a ray of unusual beauty and remarkable intensity. And yet it was not like the
sun, for it gave no heat.

The effect was excruciatingly melancholy.
Instead of a noble firmament of blue studded

with stars, there was a heavy roof of granite which seemed to crush me.

In truth we were imprisoned, bound as it were in a vast excavation. Its width was impossible to make out, the shore on either hand widening rapidly until lost to sight. Its length was equally uncertain. A haze on the distant horizon bounded our view. Looking upward, it was impossible to discover where the stupendous roof began. The lowest of the clouds must have been floating at an elevation of two thousand yards.

I use the word cavern in order to give an idea of the place. I cannot describe its awful grandeur, its savage sublimity. Whether this singular vacuum had or had not been caused by the sudden cooling of the earth when in a state of fusion, I could not say. I had read of most wonderful and gigantic caverns — but none in any way like this.

I gazed in silence. I stood upon that mysterious shore as if I were some wandering inhabitant of a distant planet. I looked on, I reflected, I admired in a state of stupefaction not altogether unmingled with fear!

After an imprisonment of forty-seven days I breathed this salty air with infinite delight.

My uncle had already got over the first surprise.

"Well, then, my boy," he said, "lean on my arm, and we will stroll along the beach."

We began to walk along the shores of this extraordinary lake. To our left were abrupt rocks, piled one upon the other. Down their sides flowed innumerable cascades, limpid and murmuring streams lost in the waters of the lake. Light vapors, which rose here and there, indicated hot springs which also poured into the lake.

When we had gone about five hundred yards, we rounded a steep promontory and found ourselves close to a lofty forest! The breeze seemed to have no effect upon the trees, which remained as motionless as if they were petrified.

We hastened forward, reached the forest, and stood beneath the trees. My surprise gave way to admiration.

I was in the presence of a very ordinary product of the earth, but of singular and gigantic proportions. My uncle unhesitatingly called them by their real name.

"A forest of mushrooms," he said in his coolest manner.

Here were thousands of white mushrooms, nearly forty feet high, with tops of equal size. Beneath them reigned a gloomy and mystic darkness.

The cold in the shade of this singular forest was intense. At length we left the spot and returned to the shores of the lake, to light and comparative warmth.

We had not gone many hundreds of yards when we came upon flowering ferns as tall as pines.

"Astonishing, magnificent, splendid!" cried my uncle. "Behold the humble plants of our garden, which in the first ages of the world were mighty trees. Harry, no botanist has ever before gazed on such a sight!"

"You are right, Uncle," I remarked. "Providence appears to have designed a vast hothouse here for preserving antediluvian plants."

"It is indeed a mighty hothouse. You would be within the bounds of reason if you also added — a vast menagerie."

I looked around anxiously. If the animals were as exaggerated as the plants, our situation would certainly be serious.

"A menagerie?"

"Doubtless. Look at the bones with which the soil of the seashore is covered — "

"Bones," I replied. "Yes, certainly, the bones of antediluvian animals."

I stooped down as I spoke, and picked up one or two relics of a bygone age.

"Here is the lower jawbone of a mastodon," I cried. "Here are the molars of the dinotherium, and here is a leg bone which belonged to the megatherium. You are right, Uncle, it is indeed a menagerie. And yet — "

"And yet, Nephew?" said my uncle, noticing that I suddenly came to a full stop.

"I do not understand the presence of such beasts in granite caverns," was my reply.

"Why not?" said my uncle with his old impatience.

"Because it is well known that animal life only existed on earth during the secondary period, when sedimentary soil was formed by the alluviums and replaced the hot and burning rocks of the primitive age."

"Harry, this *is* sedimentary soil."

"How can that be — at such enormous depth from the surface of the earth?"

"It can be explained simply. At a certain period the earth consisted of an elastic crust liable to upward and downward movements according to the law of attraction. It is probable that many a landslip in those days cast large portions of sedimentary soil into huge and mighty chasms."

"But, Uncle," I interrupted. "If antediluvian animals formerly lived in these subterraneous regions, one of those huge monsters may at this moment be concealed behind one of those rocks."

As I spoke, I looked around, examining

every point of the horizon. Nothing alive appeared to exist on these deserted shores.

I suddenly felt tired. I seated myself at the end of a promontory at the foot of which the waves broke in incessant rolls. At the extreme end was a little port protected by huge pyramids of stones. So natural did it seem that every minute I expected a ship to come out under sail and make for the open sea.

But this illusion never lasted more than a minute. We were the only living creatures in this subterranean world!

When the wind dropped, there was a silence deeper, more terrible than the silence of the desert. Amid the awful stillness, I tried to penetrate the distant fog, to tear down the veil which concealed the mysterious distance.

My uncle and I passed an hour or more in silent contemplation, then returned to the grotto. After a light meal, I sought refuge in slumber.

Launching the Raft

On the morning of the next day, to my great surprise, I awoke completely restored. Soon after rising, I plunged into the waters of this new Mediterranean. The bath was cool, fresh, and invigorating.

I came back to breakfast with an excellent appetite. Never had the coffee been so welcomed and refreshing.

When I had finished, my uncle said, "Come with me. It is high tide, and I am anxious to study i? curious manifestations here."

"Did you say tide, Uncle?"

"I did."

"Do you mean to say that the influence of the sun and moon is felt here, below?"

"Why not? Are not all bodies influenced by the law of universal attraction? Why should this underground sea be exempt from the rule of the universe? Despite the great at-

169

mospheric pressure down here, you will notice that this inland sea rises and falls with as much regularity as the Atlantic itself."

As my uncle spoke, we reached the sandy shore; the waves breaking monotonously on the beach. They were evidently rising.

"This is truly flood tide," I cried, looking at the water at my feet.

"Yes," replied my uncle, rubbing his hands with gusto. "And you can tell by these streaks of foam that the tide rises at least ten or twelve feet. It is quite natural."

"It may appear so to you, my dear uncle," was my reply, "but it is almost impossible for me to believe what I see. Who could imagine that beneath the crust of our earth there exists a real ocean with ebbing and flowing tides, with changes of winds, and even storms?"

"But, Harry, why not?" inquired my uncle. "Is there any physical reason for opposing it?"

"Well, if we give up the theory of the central heat of the earth anything should be possible."

"Then you will own," he added, "that the theories of Sir Humphrey Davy have been proven to this point?"

"I will allow that. I certainly can see no

170

reason for doubting the existence of seas and other wonders — even continents in the interior of the globe," I replied.

"That is so, but of course these continents are uninhabited?"

"I grant that it is more likely than not. Still, I do not see why this sea should not have given shelter to some species of fish."

"So far, we have not discovered any. And the probabilities are rather against it," observed the professor.

"Well, I am determined to solve the question. I shall try my luck with fishing line and hook."

"Make the experiment," said my uncle, pleased with my enthusiasm.

"By the way, what is our position now?" I asked.

"We are now three hundred and fifty leagues from Iceland," replied the professor.

"And are we still going to the southeast?"

"Yes, with a western declination of nineteen degrees. I have discovered a very curious fact."

"What is that uncle?"

"That the needle, instead of dipping toward the pole, as it does on earth in the northern hemisphere, has an upward tendency."

"This proves," I cried, "that the great

point of magnetic attraction lies somewhere between the surface of the earth and this spot we have reached."

"Exactly, my observant nephew," exclaimed my uncle.

"Well," said I, rather surprised, "this discovery will astonish experimental philosophers. It was never suspected."

"Science, great, mighty, and in the end unerring," replied my uncle, dogmatically. "Science has fallen into many errors — errors which have been fortunate and useful, for they have been the stepping-stones to truth."

After some further discussion, I turned to another matter.

"Have you any idea of the depth we have reached?" I asked.

"We are now exactly thirty-five leagues — or over a hundred miles — down into the interior of the earth."

"So," I said after measuring the distance on the map, "we are now beneath the Scottish Highlands."

"It sounds very alarming," said the professor, "but the vault which supports this vast mass of earth and rock is solid and safe."

"I have no fear that our granite sky will fall on our heads, Uncle. But are you thinking yet of going back to the surface of the earth?"

"Go back!" cried my uncle in a tone of alarm. "Surely you are not thinking of anything so absurd or cowardly. My intention is to continue our journey. We have been singularly fortunate and I hope we shall be more so."

"But how are we to cross this water?" I asked.

Oceans are, after all, only great lakes surrounded by land. Does it not stand to reason that this Central Sea is surrounded by granite?"

"Doubtless," was my natural reply.

"Well, then, do you doubt that on reaching the other side, we shall find some means of continuing our journey?"

"Probably. But how far would you say this ocean extends?"

"Well, it should extend about forty or fifty leagues."

"What then?" I asked.

"My dear boy, we have no time for further discussion. We shall embark tomorrow."

I looked around. I could see nothing in the shape of boat or vessel.

"Where, if I may ask, is the vessel to carry us?"

"It will not be exactly what you would call a vessel. For the present we must be content with a good and solid raft."

"A raft," I cried, incredulously. "But it is as impossible to construct a raft down here as a boat — "

"My good Harry, if you were to listen instead of talking you would hear," said my uncle, growing more impatient.

"I should hear what?"

"Hammering. Hans has been at work for hours."

"Making a raft?"

"Yes."

"But where has he found suitable trees?"

"Come, and we shall see."

More and more amazed, I followed my uncle.

After a walk of about a quarter of an hour, I saw Hans at work on the other side of the promontory which formed our natural port. A few minutes more and I was beside him. To my great surprise, a half-finished raft lay on the sandy shore. It was made from beams of a very peculiar wood, and a great number of pieces lay about — sufficient to have constructed a fleet of ships and boats.

I turned to my uncle, silent with astonishment and awe.

"Where did all this wood come from?" I asked. "What wood is it?"

"Well, there is pine, fir, and palm — mineralized by the action of the sea," he replied.

My uncle picked up two pieces and cast them into the sea. The pieces of wood, after having disappeared for a moment, came to the surface and floated about with the oscillation produced by wind and tide.

"Are you convinced?" said my uncle.

"I am convinced," I said, "that what I see is incredible."

My journey into the interior of the earth was rapidly changing all preconceived notions, and day by day preparing me for more marvels.

The very next evening, thanks to Hans, the raft was finished. It was about ten feet long and five feet wide. The beams, bound together with stout ropes, were solid and firm. Once launched, the improvised vessel floated tranquilly on the waters of what the professor had well named the Central Sea.

... On the Waters—
a Raft Voyage

On the fifteenth of August we were up early.
At six o'clock in the morning, when the
eager professor gave the signal to embark,
the food, the luggage, all our instruments,
our weapons, and a good supply of sweet
water, which we had collected from springs
in the rocks, were placed on the raft.

Hans had made a rudder, which enabled
him to guide the floating apparatus with
ease. He took the tiller, as a matter of course,
for he was as good a sailor as he was a guide.
I then let go the painter which held us to
the shore. The sail was brought into the wind,
and we moved rapidly offshore. Once more
we were making for distant and unknown
regions.

Just as we were about to leave the little
port, my uncle, who was keen on geographical names, suggested naming the port for me.

"I have another idea," I said. "I should like to call it Gretchen. Port Gretchen will look very well on our future map."

"Then Port Gretchen it shall be," said the professor.

Thus it was that the memory of my dear girl became part of our auspicious expedition.

When we left the shore, we sailed directly before the wind at a much greater speed than might have been expected from a raft.

At the end of an hour, my uncle, who had been making careful observations, was able to judge the speed with which we moved. It was far beyond any speed on earth.

"If," he said, "we continue to advance at our present rate, we shall travel at least thirty leagues in twenty-four hours. This is an almost incredible velocity for a raft."

Without making any reply, I went forward on the raft. Already the shore was fading away on the edge of the horizon. Before me I could see nothing but the vast and apparently limitless sea upon which we floated, the only living objects in sight.

Huge and dark clouds cast their gray shadows below, shadows which seemed to crush that colorless and sullen water by their weight. Anything more suggestive of gloom and of regions of nether darkness, I never beheld. Silvery rays of electric light, reflected here and there upon some small spots of water, brought up luminous sparkles in the long wake of our cumbrous bark. Presently we were wholly out of sight of land; not a vestige could be seen, nor any indication of where we were going. So still and motionless did we seem, without any distant point to fix our eyes on, that but for the phosphoric light at the wake of the raft I should have fancied that we were still and motionless.

But I knew that we were advancing at a very rapid rate.

About twelve o'clock in the day, we discovered vast masses of seaweed floating around us on all sides. Our raft swept past great specimens of marine algae, some from three to four thousand feet in length, looking like snakes uncoiling out far beyond our horizon. Hour after hour passed before we came to the end of these floating weeds.

At length night came, but the luminous state of the atmosphere did not diminish. As soon as our supper had been disposed of, I stretched out at the foot of the mast and went to sleep.

Hans remained motionless at the tiller.

The wind being aft and the sail square, all he had to do was to keep his oar in the center.

My uncle had directed me to keep a log, and to put down even the most minute particulars of our extraordinary voyage from the time we departed Port Gretchen.

From our log, therefore, I tell the story of our voyage on the Central Sea.

Friday, August 16th. A steady breeze from the northwest. Raft progressing with extreme rapidity, and going perfectly straight. Coast about thirty leagues to leeward. Nothing to be seen ahead but the horizon. The intensity of the light neither increases nor diminishes. The weather remarkably fine; light and fleecy clouds, surrounded by an atmosphere resembling melted silver.

Thermometer about 32.2° Centigrade (90° F.).

About twelve o'clock in the day, Hans cast his fishing line into the subterranean waters. The bait he used was a small piece of meat. When a sudden and rather hard tug came on the line, Hans drew it in — and with it a fish.

"It is a sturgeon!" I cried. "Certainly a small sturgeon."

The professor examined the fish carefully.

"This fish, my dear boy, belongs to a family which has been extinct for ages. Its fossil remains have been found in the Devonian strata."

"You mean to say," I cried, "that we have captured a live specimen of a fish that existed in the primitive sea?"

"We have," said the professor.

"But to what family does it belong?"

"To the order Ganoides — of the family Cephalaspides, of the genus Pterychtis — yes, I am certain of it. This fish exhibits a peculiarity known only in fish that live in subterranean waters. It is blind."

"Blind!" I cried, much surprised.

"Not only blind," continued the professor, "but absolutely without eyes."

I now examined our discovery for myself. It was a fact. This, however, might be a solitary case, I suggested. The hook was baited again and once more thrown into the water. In two hours we caught a large number of Pterychtis, as well as other fish. All, without exception, were blind. This unexpected capture renewed our stock of provisions very satisfactorily.

We were now convinced that this subterranean sea contained only fish known to us as fossil specimens.

I took the telescope and carefully examined the horizon. It was utterly and entirely deserted. I gazed for some time on the strange and mysterious sky. And though I could neither see nor discover anything, my imagination carried me away.

In a kind of waking dream, I thought I saw on the surface of the water enormous antediluvian turtles as big as floating islands. On those dull and somber shores passed a ghostly row of the mammals of early days: the great Leptotherium found in the Brazilian hills, the Mesicotherium, a native of the glacial regions of Siberia.

Farther on, I thought I saw the gigantic tapir ready to do battle for its prey with the Anoplotherium, a strange animal resembling at the same time a rhinoceros, a horse, a hippopotamus, and a camel.

There was the giant mastodon, twisting and turning his huge trunk, while the Megatherium, his enormous claws stretched out, dug into the earth for food.

Higher up clambered the first monkey ever seen on the face of the globe. Still farther away ran the Pterodactyl, with the winged hand, gliding through the compressed air like a huge bat.

Above all, in the leaden sky, were immense

birds, which spread their mighty wings and fluttered against the huge stone vault of the inland sea.

My dream was of countless ages before the existence of man. I passed like a shadow in the midst of brushwood as lofty as the giant trees of California. I leaned against the huge columnlike trunks of giant trees to which those of Canada were as ferns. Whole ages passed, hundreds upon hundreds of years were concentrated into a single day.

What an extraordinary dream! I had during this period of hallucination forgotten everything — the professor, the guide, and the raft on which we were floating. My mind was in a state of semioblivion.

"What is the matter, Harry?" said my uncle, suddenly.

My eyes, which were wide opened like those of a somnambulist, were fixed upon him, but I did not see him nor could I clearly make out anything around me.

"Take care, my boy," cried my uncle. "You will fall into the sea."

As he uttered these words, I felt myself seized by Hans. Had it not been for him, I would have fallen into the waves and been drowned.

"Have you gone mad?" cried my uncle, shaking me.

"What — what is the matter?" I said at last, coming to myself.

"Are you ill, Harry?" continued the professor anxiously.

"No — no; but I have had an extraordinary dream," I said, looking around me with strangely puzzled eyes. "All seems well," I added.

"All is well," said my uncle; "a beautiful breeze, a splendid sea. If I am not out in my calculations, we shall soon see land, my boy!"

As my uncle uttered these words, I carefully scanned the horizon. But the line of water in the distance was still obscured in lowering clouds.

Terrific Saurian Combat

Saturday, August 17th. No land in sight.

I cannot banish from my mind my extraordinary dream.

The professor is in one of his morose humors. Spends his time in scanning the horizon at every point of the compass.

"You seem uneasy, Uncle," I said, when for about the hundredth time he put down his telescope and walked up and down muttering to himself.

"No, I am not uneasy," he replied, "but impatient. I am annoyed to find the sea so much vaster than I expected."

I then recollected that the professor had estimated the width of this subterranean ocean at about thirty leagues. We had already traveled over three times that distance without discovering any trace of the distant shore. I began to understand my uncle's anger.

"We are not going *down*," exclaimed the professor. "All this is utter loss of time."

"But," I argued, "if we have followed the route indicated by Saknussemm, we cannot be going far wrong."

"That is the question. Are we following the route taken by that wondrous sage? Did Saknussemm ever come upon this great sheet of water? If he did, did he cross it?"

"In any case, it is something to have seen this magnificent spectacle," I said.

"I care nothing about magnificent spectacles," my uncle replied. "I came down into the interior of the earth with one object, and that object I mean to attain."

After this I thought it best to hold my tongue.

At six o'clock in the evening Hans asked for his week's salary, and receiving his rixdollars put them carefully in his pocket. He was perfectly contented.

Sunday, August 18th. My uncle has tried deep-sea soundings. He tied the cross of one of our heaviest crowbars to the end of a cord, which he ran out to two hundred fathoms.

When the crowbar was dragged back on board, Hans called my attention to some singular marks on its surface. The piece of iron looked as if it had been crushed between two very hard substances.

I looked at our guide with an inquiring glance.

"Tander," said he. Hans opened his mouth once or twice as if in the act of biting, and in this way made me understand his meaning.

"Teeth!" I cried, with stupefaction, as I examined the bar of iron with more attention.

Yes, the indentations on the bar of iron are the marks of teeth! Is my dream about to come true? A dread and terrible reality!

All day my thoughts were bent upon these speculations.

Monday, August 19th. I have been trying to remember the particular characteristics of the animals of the secondary period — those which preceded the mammals. At that time, reptiles reigned supreme on earth. These hideous monsters ruled everything in the seas of the secondary period.

The existing Saurians, which include all such reptiles as lizards, crocodiles, and alligators, even the largest and most formidable, are feeble imitations of the animals of ages long ago. If there were giants in the days of old, there were also gigantic animals.

From their fossil bones, we have reconstructed them to get some idea of their colossal formation. I once saw the skeleton of one of these wonderful Saurians in the museum of Hamburg. It measured no less than thirty feet from the nose to the tail. Was I destined to find myself face to face with these monsters? I stared wildly and with terror at the subterranean sea. Every moment I expected one of those creatures to rise from the vast, cavernous depths.

I fancied that the professor shared my notion, for after an attentive examination of the crowbar he cast his eyes rapidly over the ocean.

I thought, "No doubt we have disturbed some terrible monster in his watery home, and we may pay dearly for our boldness."

Anxious to be prepared for the worst, I examined our weapons and saw that they were ready for use. My uncle looked at me and nodded his head approvingly.

At that moment, surface waters indicated that something was in motion below. Was danger approaching? We had to keep watch.

Tuesday, August 20th. Evening comes at last. At least the desire to sleep makes our eyelids heavy, for there is no night darkness in this place. Hans remains at the tiller. When or if he sleeps, I cannot say. I take advantage of his vigilance to get some rest.

Two hours later I was awakened by an awful shock. The raft appeared to have struck a sunken rock. It was lifted right out of the water by some mysterious power and then deposited some twenty fathoms away.

"What is it?" cried my uncle, starting up. "Are we shipwrecked or what?"

Hans pointed to where, about two hundred yards off, a huge black mass was moving up and down. I looked with awe. My worst fears were realized.

"It is a colossal monster!" I cried.

"Yes," cried the agitated professor. "It is a huge sea lizard of terrible size and shape. And farther on is an enormous crocodile. Will you look at his hideous jaws and that row of monstrous teeth!"

We stare, stupefied and terror-stricken at the sight of this fearful marine monster that could crush our raft and ourselves with a single bite.

Hans seizes the tiller which has twisted out of his hand, and puts it hard aweather to hasten our escape. But, no sooner does he do so, than he sees to leeward a turtle about forty feet wide, and a serpent quite as long, whose enormous, hideous head is peering out of the waters.

Turn which way we will, it is impossible for us to flee. The fearful reptiles advance upon us. They twist about the raft with awful speed, making a series of concentric circles around us. I take up my rifle. But what effect can a rifle ball have on the scaly armor which covers the bodies of those horrid monsters?

We remain still and dumb from utter horror. The monsters come steadily closer. Our fate appears certain, fearful, and terrible. On one side the mighty crocodile; on the other the great sea serpent. (The lizard, fortunately, has plunged beneath the briny waves and disappeared.)

I am about to try the effect of firing a shot when Hans signals to me. The two hideous and ravenous monsters pass within fifty fathoms of the raft, and then make a rush. Their fury and rage at one another prevent them from seeing us.

As the combat commences, we can distinctly make out every action of the two hideous monsters.

The first has the snout of a porpoise, the head of a lizard, the teeth of a crocodile.

"It is the most fearful of all antediluvian reptiles — the Ichthyosaurus, or great fish lizard," said my uncle.

"The other is a monstrous serpent concealed under the hard vaulted shell of the turtle. It is the terrible enemy of its fearful rival, and is called the Plesiosaurus, or sea crocodile.

I see the flaming red eyes of the Ichthyosaurus, each as big or bigger than a man's head. This one measures not less than a hundred feet in length, and I can form some idea of his girth when I see him lift his prodigious tail out of the water. His jaw is of awful size and strength, and according to the best informed naturalists, it contains a hundred and eighty-two teeth.

The other, Plesiosaurus, is a serpent with a cylindrical trunk, a short stumpy tail, and fins like a bank of oars in a Roman gallery. Its whole body is covered by a carapace, or shell, and its neck, as flexible as that of a swan, rises more than thirty feet above the waves — a tower of animated flesh!

These animals attacked one another with inconceivable fury. Such a combat was never seen before by mortal eyes. To us who did see it, it appeared more like the phantasmagoric creation of a dream than anything else. They raised mountains of water that dashed in spray over the raft, which was already tossed to and fro by the waves. Twenty times we seemed on the point of being upset and hurled headlong into the waves. Hideous hisses shook the gloomy granite roof of that mighty cavern and carried terror to our hearts.

One hour, two hours, three hours passed — the struggle continued without result. The deadly opponents now approached, now drew away from the raft. Once or twice we fancied they were about to leave us, but then they came nearer and nearer.

We crouched on the raft, ready to fire at them at a moment's notice.

Suddenly they disappeared beneath the waves, leaving behind them a maelstrom in the midst of the sea. We were very nearly sucked down in this whirlpool.

Several minutes passed before we saw anything further. Was this awesome combat to end in the depths of the ocean?

Then, a short distance from us, an enormous mass rose out of the water — the head of the great Plesiosaurus. The terrible monster was mortally wounded. I could see nothing of his enormous body, but his serpent-like neck twisted and curled in all the agonies of death. His neck struck the water like a gigantic whip, and then wriggled like a worm cut in two. Soon his movements slackened visibly, his contortions almost ceased. At last the body of the mighty snake lay, an inert, dead mass, on the surface of the now calm and placid waters.

"As for the Ichthyosaurus?" I asked myself. "Has he gone down to his mighty cavern under the sea to rest, or will he reappear to destroy us?"

This question remained unanswered. But now, at least, we had some breathing time.

The Sea Monster

Wednesday, August 21st. Fortunately the wind moved us away from the location of the struggle.

Our voyage now became monotonous. But I had no desire to have it broken by any repetition of yesterday.

Thursday, August 22nd. The wind is now NNE and has changed to fitful gusts. The temperature is high. We are now moving at the average rate of about ten and a half miles per hour.

About twelve o'clock we heard a distant sound, like thunder, only that it was one continuous roar.

"Far off in the distance," explained the professor, "there must be some rock or some island against which the sea is breaking violently."

Hans climbed the mast, but could see nothing. The ocean lay smooth in every direction.

Three hours passed without any sign to indicate what might be before us. Then the sound began to assume the roar of a mighty cataract.

Are we moving toward some mighty waterfall which shall cast us into the abyss? Probably this would be agreeable to the professor because it would be something like the vertical descent he is so eager to make. I entertain a very different opinion.

Whatever it is though, it must be some very extraordinary phenomenon, for as we advance the roar becomes stupendous. Is it in the water or in the air?

I cast hasty glances aloft, but the vault above is tranquil. The clouds appear utterly still and motionless, lost in the irradiation of electric light.

I examine the horizon. Its aspect still remains unchanged. But if these tremendous roars are produced by the noise of falling water, the current would increase in activity. I check the current. It simply does not exist;

an empty bottle cast into the water lies to leeward without motion.

About four o'clock Hans again climbs the mast, this time to the crow's nest. From this elevated position he looks around.

At last his eyes remain fixed. His face expresses no astonishment but his eyes widen slightly.

"He has seen something!" cried my uncle.

"I think so," I replied.

Hans came down, stood beside us, and pointed to the south.

"Der nere," he said.

"There," replied my uncle. And seizing his telescope he looked through it for about a minute, which to me seemed an age.

"Yes, yes," he cried, in a tone of considerable surprise. "There it is."

"What?" I asked.

"A tremendous spurt of water rising out of the waves."

"Some other marine monster?" I asked, already alarmed.

"Perhaps."

"Then let us steer more to the westward, for we know what we can expect from antediluvian animals."

"No, let us go ahead," said my uncle.

I turned toward Hans. He was at the tiller steering with his usual calm. And I re-minded myself that we left caution behind when we first entered the underworld.

Accordingly, we continued to advance. The nearer we come, the loftier is the spouting water. What monster can fill himself with such huge volumes of water?

At eight o'clock in the evening we are not more than two leagues from the mighty beast. Its long, black, mountainous body lies on the top of the water like an island. Sailors have mistaken whales for islands. Is this too an illusion? But its length cannot be less than a thousand fathoms! What, then, *is* this monster?

It is quite motionless. The sea seems unable to lift it upwards. The waves are breaking on its huge and gigantic frame. The waterspout, rising to a height of five hundred feet, breaks in spray with a dull, sullen roar.

We advance like senseless lunatics toward this mighty mass.

I honestly confess that I was abjectly afraid. I threatened in my terror to cut the sheet of the sail. I attacked the professor, calling him foolhardy, mad — I know not what. He made no answer.

Suddenly Hans pointed toward the menacing object.

"Holme!"

"An island!" cried my uncle.

"An island!" I was angry at this poor attempt at deception.

"Of course it is," cried my uncle, bursting into a loud and joyous laugh.

"But the waterspout?"

"Geyser," said Hans.

"Yes, of course, a geyser," replied my uncle, still laughing.

At a distance the island presented the appearance of an enormous whale whose head rose high above the water. The geyser, a word which signifies fury, rose majestically from its summit.

"Let us go on shore," said the professor, after some minutes of silence.

Hans steered to the extreme end of the island.

I was the first to leap on the rock. My uncle followed, while Hans remained on the raft. We soon came in sight of the little central basin from which the geyser rose. I plunged a thermometer into the water which boiled out of the center; it registered a heat of a hundred and sixty-three degrees (325° Fahrenheit).

This water, therefore, came from some-place where the heat was intense. This contradicted the theories of Professor Hardwigg. I could not help telling him so.

"So," he answered sharply, "what does that prove against my doctrine?"

"Nothing," I replied, seeing that I was banging my head against a stone wall.

Nevertheless, it appears evident that we shall sooner or later arrive at a region where the heat will reach its utmost limits, far beyond the measurement of thermometers.

Visions of Hades, which the ancients believed to be in the center of the earth, float through my mind.

We shall see what we shall see. That is the professor's favorite phrase now. Having christened the volcanic island after me, my uncle turned away and gave the signal to return to the raft.

I stood still, however, for some minutes longer, gazing upon the magnificent geyser. The upward tendency of the water was irregular; it diminished in intensity, then regained new vigor. I attributed this to the variation of the pressure of the accumulated vapors in its reservoir.

Before we took our final departure from

the island, I calculated the distance we had gone for my journal. Since we left Port Gretchen, we had traveled two hundred and seventy leagues — more than eight hundred miles — on this great inland sea. We were therefore six hundred and twenty leagues from Iceland, and exactly under England.

The Battle of the Elements

Friday, August 23rd. This morning the magnificent geyser has wholly disappeared. The wind had freshened, and we are fast leaving the neighborhood of Harry's Island, as my uncle had baptized it.

The weather, if we may use such an expression, is about to change. The atmosphere is loaded with vapors, which carry with them electricity formed by the constant evaporation of the salty waters. The clouds are lowering noticeably and are taking on a dark olive hue. Another and terrible drama is soon to be enacted. This time it is not to be a contest between animals, but a fearful battle of the elements.

Cumulus clouds, the towering clouds often seen before a storm, are piled in the south. The air is heavy; the sea is unusually calm.

One can feel that the entire atmosphere is saturated with electricity. My hair literally stands on end, as if under the influence of a galvanic battery. If one of my companions ventured to touch me, I think he would receive a violent shock.

About ten o'clock in the morning, the signs of the storm became definite; the wind seemed to slacken as if to take breath for a violent attack. A great silence prevailed. Nature assumed a dead calm — and ceased to breathe.

On the mast, the sail hangs in loose, heavy folds. The raft is motionless in the midst of the dark, heavy sea — without undulation, without motion. It is as still as glass. As we are making no progress what is the use of keeping up the sail?

"Let us lower the sail," I said; "it is the only prudent thing to do."

"No — no," cried my uncle, in an exasperated tone. "Let the wind strike us and do its worst. Let the storm sweep us away where it will — only let me see the glimmer of some coast, some rocky cliff, even if it dash our raft into a thousand pieces. No! keep the sail up!"

These words were scarcely uttered when the southern horizon underwent a sudden violent change. The air became a wild and raging tempest.

It came from the most distant corners of the mighty cavern. It raged from every point of the compass. It roared, it yelled, it shrieked with glee as of demons let loose. The darkness increased and became indeed darkness visible.

The raft rose and fell with the storm, and bounded over the waves. My uncle was thrown headlong on the deck. With great difficulty I dragged myself toward him. He was holding on tightly to the end of a rope, and appeared to be enjoying the spectacle of the unchained elements.

Hans barely moved a muscle. His long hair, driven hither and thither by the tempest, and scattered wildly over his motionless face, gave him a most extraordinary appearance, for his hair-ends danced with sparks of electricity.

Still the mast holds against the storm. The sail spreads out and fills like a soap bubble about to burst. The raft pushes on at a pace impossible to estimate.

"The sail, the sail!" I cried, endeavoring to lower it.

"Let it alone!" says my uncle, more exasperated than ever.

"Nej," says Hans, gently shaking his head at me.

The rain formed a roaring cataract in front of the horizon, to which we were rushing like madmen.

Before this wilderness of water reached us, the mighty veil of cloud was torn in two and the sea began to foam wildly. Fearful claps of thunder followed dazzling flashes of lightning such as I had never seen. The flashes came from every side, crossing one another, as the thunder peeled and echoed. The mass of vapor becomes incandescent. Hailstones strike the metal of our boots; our weapons are actually luminous. The waves as they rise appear to be fire-eating monsters, their crests surmounted by combs of flame.

My eyes are dazzled, blinded by the intensity of light, my ears are deafened by the awful roar of the elements. I hold onto the mast, which bends like a reed beneath the violence of the storm . . .

Sunday, August 25th. Where have we got to? In what region are we wandering? We are still carried forward with inconceivable speed.

The night has been fearful, something not to be described. The storm shows no sign of letting up. We exist in the midst of an uproar which has no name. The detonations which sound like artillery are incessant. Our ears literally bleed. We are unable to exchange a word or hear each other speak.

The lightning never ceases to flash for a single instant. The forked streaks plunge in every direction and take the form of globes of fire, which explode like bombshells over a beleaguered city.

There is a constant emission of light from the storm clouds. Innumerable columns of water rush up like waterspouts and fall upon the surface of the ocean in foam.

Whither are we going? My uncle still lies at full length upon the raft, without speaking.

The heat increases.

Monday, August 26th. This terrible storm will never end.

We are utterly broken by fatigue. The raft is running to the southeast. We have now already traveled two hundred leagues from Harry's Island.

About twelve o'clock the storm becomes worse than ever. We tied ourselves to the mast, each man lashing the other. The waves drove over us, so that several times we were actually underwater.

We open our mouths, we move our lips, but no sound comes. Even when we place our mouths to each other's ears, it is the same. The wind carries the voice away.

My uncle once contrived to get his head close to mine after several vain endeavors. I had a notion, it was more intuition than anything else, that he said to me, "We are lost."

I took my notebook from my pocket and wrote a few words as legibly as I could: "Take in sail."

With a deep sigh he nodded and acquiesced.

A moment later, a ball of fire appears on the very edge of the raft. The mast and sail are carried away and I see them rise like a kite.

We are frozen with terror. The ball of fire, half white, half azure-colored and about the size of a ten-inch bombshell, moves along with a frightful rapidity to leeward of the storm. It clambers up one of the bulwarks of the raft, up on the sack of provisions, and finally falls lightly, like a football, on our powder barrel.

Horrible situation! An explosion is inevitable.

By heaven's mercy it was not so.

The dazzling disc moved to one side. It

approached Hans, who stared at it. Then it approached my uncle, who fell on his knees to avoid it. It came toward me, as I stood pale and shuddering in its dazzling light and heat, and pirouetted round my feet.

An odor of nitrous gas filled the whole air; it penetrated to my throat, to my lungs. I felt ready to choke.

Why is it that I cannot withdraw my feet? Are they riveted to the flooring of the raft?

No.

The electric globe has turned all the iron on board into lodestone — the instruments, the tools, the guns, are clanging together with an awful noise. The nails of my heavy boots adhere to the plate of iron incrustated in the wood. I cannot withdraw my feet.

At last, by superhuman effort, I tear myself away just as the ball, executing its gyratory motions, is about to engulf me. . . .

Oh, what intense stupendous light! The globe of fire bursts — we are enveloped in cascades of living fire!

Then it all goes out. But before darkness once more covers the scene, I have just time enough to see my uncle thrown on the flooring of the raft and Hans "spitting fire" under the influence of the electricity which seemed to have passed through him.

Where are we going? Oh, where are we going?

Tuesday, August 27th. I have just come out of a long fainting fit. The awful storm continues. The lightning has increased and pours out its fiery wrath like a brood of serpents let loose in the atmosphere.

Are we still upon the sea? Yes, and being carried along with incredible velocity.

We have passed under England, under the Channel, under France, probably under all of Europe.

Another awful clamor in the distance. This time it is certain that, close by, the sea is breaking upon rock. Then —

Our Route Reversed

Here ends my journal of our voyage on the raft; happily it was saved from the wreck.

What happened when the terrible shock took place? When the raft was cast up on the rocky shore? It would be impossible for me now to say. I felt myself thrown backward into the boiling waves, and I escaped certain death because Hans held me by the arm.

The courageous Icelander carried me out of the reach of the waves and laid me down on a burning expanse of sand, where I found myself sometime afterwards in the company of my uncle.

Then Hans quietly returned to the rocks in order to save what he could from the wreck. I could not utter a word. I felt drained of feeling and bruised and broken with fatigue. It took hours for me to recover.

Meanwhile the fearful deluge of rain continued to fall, its very violence proclaiming the approaching end of the storm. Some overhanging rocks gave us a little protection from the torrent.

Under this shelter Hans prepared some food, but I was unable to touch it. Exhausted by three weary days and nights of watching, we then fell into a deep sleep.

Next day when I awoke, the change was magical. The weather was magnificent. Air and sea had regained their serenity. I was greeted on awakening by the first joyous tones I had heard from the professor for many a day.

"Well, my lad," he cried. "Have you slept soundly?"

You would think to hear him, that we were back in the old house on the Konigstrasse, that I had just come down quietly to my breakfast, and that my marriage with Gretchen was to take place that very day. When, in fact, considering that the tempest had probably driven us eastward, we had passed under the whole of Germany, under the city of Hamburg where I had been so happy, and under the very street which contained all I loved and cared for in the world.

All these dreary and miserable reflections went through my mind before I answered my uncle's question.

"What is the matter?" he cried. "Can you not say whether you have slept well or not?"

"I have slept very well; every bone in my body aches, but I suppose it's nothing serious."

"Nothing at all, my boy. It is only the result of the fatigue of the last few days, that is all."

"You appear to be very jolly this morning," I said.

"Delighted, my dear boy, delighted. We have at last reached the wished-for port."

"The end of our expedition?" I cried, hopefully.

"No, but the end of that sea which I began to fear would never end. We will now resume our journey by land, and once again endeavor to dive into the center of the earth."

"My dear uncle, allow me to ask you one question."

"Certainly, Harry. A dozen, if you like."

"One will suffice. How will we get back?" I asked.

"How will we get back? What a question to ask! We have not yet reached the end."

"I know that. All I want to know is how you propose to return?"

"In the most simple way in the world," said the professor. "Once we reach the exact center of the earth, either we shall find a new road by which to ascend to the surface, or we shall simply go back the way we came. I have reason to believe that it will not close behind us."

"Then one of the first things to see to is the repair of the raft," was my melancholy response.

"Of course."

"Then comes the all-important question of provisions," I urged. "Have we enough left to enable us to accomplish this great design you contemplate?"

"I have already looked into this. Hans is a very clever fellow. He has saved the greater part of the cargo. Come and judge for yourself."

My uncle led the way out of the shelter. When we reached the shore, we found Hans standing in the midst of a large number of salvaged things laid out in complete order.

This man, whose devotion to his employers

211

I never saw surpassed, had succeeded in saving the most precious articles of our cargo.

Of course we did suffer several severe losses. Our weapons had vanished, but the gunpowder, from which we narrowly escaped death in the storm, was saved.

"Well," said the professor, "as we have no guns, we have to give up the idea of hunting."

"What about our instruments?"

"Here is the manometer, the most useful of all. With it alone I can calculate the depth, and decide when we have reached the center of the earth. Ha, ha! But for this little instrument we might make a mistake and run the risk of coming out at the antipodes!"

"But the compass," I said. "Without that what can we do?"

"Here it is!" he cried, with real joy. "And here we have the chronometer and the thermometers."

As far as the instruments were concerned, nothing was wanting. I also found ladders, ropes, pickaxes, crowbars, and shovels — all scattered about on the shore.

There was, however, the most important question of all — provisions.

"But what are we to do for food?" I asked.

"Let us see," replied my uncle, gravely.

The boxes which contained our supply of food for the voyage were in a good state of preservation — biscuits, salt meat, schiedam, and dried fish.

"About four months supply!" cried the professor, in high glee. "Then we shall have plenty of time to go and to come, and with what remains I plan to give a grand dinner for my colleagues when we get home."

I sighed. The temperament of my uncle astonished me more and more every day.

"Now," he said, "before we do anything else we must lay in a stock of fresh water. The rain has filled the hollows of the granite. There is a fine supply of water. I shall ask Hans to repair the raft as best he can, though I believe we shall not require it again."

"How so?" I asked.

"I have an idea, my dear boy, that we shall not come out the same way we entered."

Little did I think how true and prophetic his words were.

"And now," he said, "to breakfast."

With dried meat, biscuit, and a delicious cup of tea, we made a satisfactory meal. While we were eating, I asked my uncle how we now stood in relation to the world above.

"If we were compelled to fix the exact spot," said my uncle, "it might be difficult, since I could keep no record of our speed or direction during the storm. Still, we will endeavor to approximate to the truth. We should not be so very far out."

"If I reflected rightly," I replied, "our last observation was made at the geyser island."

"Harry's Island, my boy! Harry's Island. Do not decline the honor of giving your name to an island discovered by us — the first human beings to walk on it since the creation of the world!"

"Very well. At Harry's Island we had already covered over two hundred and seventy miles of sea, and we were about six hundred leagues, more or less, from Iceland."

"Good. Let us count four days of storm, when we must have gone about eighty leagues every twenty-four hours."

I thought this a fair calculation. Thus there were three hundred leagues to be added to the grand total.

"The Central Sea must extend at least six hundred leagues from side to side. Do you know, my boy that we have discovered a sea larger than the Mediterranean?"

"Certainly. And we only know its extent in one place. It may be hundreds of miles in another."

"Very likely."

"And," said I, after calculating for some

minutes, "we are at this moment exactly under the Mediterranean."

"Do you think so?"

"I am almost certain of it. Are we not nine hundred leagues from Reykjavik?"

"That is perfectly true. But that we are under the Mediterranean and not Turkey or the Atlantic Ocean can only be determined when we are sure of not having deviated from our course."

"I do not think we were driven very far off course. The wind appeared to me to be always about the same. In my opinion this shore is situated southeast of Port Gretchen."

"I hope so. It will be easy to decide the matter by taking our bearings with the compass. Come along."

The professor walked eagerly in the direction of the rock where Hans had placed the instruments for safety. My uncle was positively lighthearted. I had never known him to be so amiable and pleasant. I followed him.

As soon as we had reached the rock, my uncle took the compass, placed it horizontally before him, and looked at the needle.

As he had at first shaken it, it oscillated considerably before assuming its right position under the influence of the magnetic power.

The professor, bent over the instrument, started violently. He closed his eyes, rubbed them, and took another, keener look.

Then he turned slowly around to me, stupefaction written on his face.

"What is the matter?" I asked, becoming alarmed.

He could not speak. He was too overwhelmed for words. He simply pointed to the instrument.

I examined it eagerly, according to his mute directions, and a loud cry of surprise escaped my lips. The needle of the compass pointed due north — in the direction we expected was south!

It pointed to the shore instead of to the sea.

I shook the compass. I examined it with anxious eyes. No defect in any way explained the phenomenon. Whatever position we forced the needle to, it returned invariably to the same unexpected point.

It was useless to conceal the fatal truth from ourselves.

Unwelcome as the fact was, there could be no doubt that during the tempest there had been a sudden shift of wind. We had been carried back to the shores we had left so many days before!

A Voyage of Discovery

It would be altogether impossible to convey the utter astonishment which overcame the professor on making this extraordinary discovery. Amazement, incredulity, and rage were so blended as to alarm me greatly.

I had never seen a man so crestfallen, then so furiously indignant.

We had to begin all over again. Instead of progressing, we had retreated.

Presently the indomitable energy of my uncle overcame every other consideration.

"So," he said, "the elements themselves conspire to overwhelm me; air, fire, and water combine to oppose my passage. Well, they shall see what the will of a determined man can do. I will not yield. I will not retreat even one inch. We shall see who shall triumph in this great contest — man or nature."

Standing upright on a rock, irritated and menacing, Professor Hardwigg seemed to defy the fates.

"Listen to me, Uncle," I said firmly, "there must be some limit to ambition here. It is utterly useless to struggle against the impossible. Pray, listen to reason. We are utterly unprepared for a sea voyage. It is simple madness to think of sailing six hundred leagues on a wretched pile of beams, with a bedspread for a sail, a paltry stick for a mast, and a tempest to contend with. As we are totally incapable of steering the raft, we shall become the mere plaything of the storm. It is acting the part of madmen to run such risks on this dangerous and treacherous Central Sea a second time."

The professor did not hear a word of my eloquence. "To the raft!" he cried, in a hoarse voice, when I paused.

I tried again. I begged and implored him. I got angry. But I had to deal with a will more determined than my own.

Hans, meanwhile, had been repairing the raft. By means of some fragments of rope, he had again made the raft seaworthy. He had hoisted a new mast and sail, the latter already fluttering and waving in the breeze.

The professor spoke a few words to our guide, who immediately began to put our baggage on board and prepare for our departure. The atmosphere was clear, and the northeast wind blew steadily. It appeared likely to last for some time.

What could I do? In a mood of sullen resignation, I was about to take my accustomed place on the raft when my uncle placed his hand upon my shoulder.

"There is no hurry, my boy," he said. "We shall not start until tomorrow. As fate has cast me upon these shores, I shall not leave without having completely examined them."

I must explain that though we had been driven back to the northern shore, we had landed at a very different spot from that which had been our starting point.

We calculated that Port Gretchen must be far to the westward.

Leaving Hans to his work, we started on our expedition. As we trudged along, our feet crushed innumerable shells of every shape and size — once the dwelling place of animals of every period of creation.

I noticed some enormous shells — carapaces (turtle and tortoise species) the diameter of which exceeded fifteen feet.

The entire soil was covered by a vast quantity of stony relics, lying in successive layers one above the other. I came to the conclusion that in past ages the sea must have covered the whole area.

I had no doubt that this mysterious sea, through imperceptible fissures, had been fed by the ocean above.

These fissures must now be clearly choked up, for if not, the cavern would have been completely filled in a short space of time. Perhaps this water, having to contend with the accumulated subterraneous fires of the interior of the earth, had even become partially vaporized. That would explain the heavy clouds suspended over our heads, and the electricity which occasioned such terrible storms in this cavernous sea.

The professor, who was now in his element, carefully examined every rocky fissure.

For a whole mile we followed the windings of the Central Sea, when suddenly an important change took place in the appearance of the soil. It seemed to have been cast up by a violent upheaval of the lower strata.

We advanced with great difficulty over

broken granite and other alluvial deposits when a field, almost an entire *plain* of bones, appeared suddenly before our eyes! It looked like an immense cemetery, where generation after generation had mingled their mortal dust.

On that spot, some three square miles in extent, was accumulated the whole history of animal life. We were drawn forward by an all-absorbing curiosity. Our feet crushed with a dry and crackling sound the remains of those prehistoric fossils over which the museums of great cities quarrel for possession, even when they are only broken fragments.

My uncle stood for some minutes with his arms raised toward the thick granite vault which served us for a sky. His eyes sparkled wildly behind his spectacles, while his whole attitude expressed unbounded astonishment.

He stood in the presence of an endless, wondrous, and inexhaustibly rich collection of antediluvian monsters, piled up for his own private and peculiar satisfaction.

For some time he stood literally aghast at the magnitude of his discovery.

But there was even greater excitement when, darting wildly over this mass of organic dust, he caught up a naked skull and addressed me in a quivering voice.

"Harry, my boy — Harry — this is a human head!"

"A human head, Uncle!" I said, no less amazed than he.

"Yes, Nephew. Ah! Mr. Milne-Edwards, Mr. De Quatrefages, to think that you are not here where I am — I, Professor Hardwigg!"

Discovery upon Discovery

In order fully to understand my uncle's allusions to these illustrious and learned men, it will be necessary to offer certain explanations.

On the twenty-eighth of March, 1863, some laborers under the direction of Mr. Boucher of Perthes were at work in the great quarries of Moulin-Quignon, near Abbeville in France. While at work they unexpectedly came upon a human jawbone buried in fourteen feet of soil. It was the first fossil of its kind that had ever been found. Near this unexpected human relic were found stone hatchets and carved flints.

The report of this discovery spread over France, England, and Germany. Many learned men, among them the Messrs. Milne-Edwards and De Quatrefages, believed in the authenticity of the bone in question and became — to use the phrase then popular in

England — the most ardent supporters of the "jawbone question."

To the eminent geologists of the United Kingdom who supported the "jawbone question" — Messrs. Falconer, Buck, Carpenter, and others — were soon united the learned men of Germany. And among these, the most enthusiastic was my uncle, Professor Hardwigg.

The authenticity of a human fossil of the Quaternary period thus seemed to be accepted by even the most skeptical. This school of thought, however, had a bitter adversary in Mr. Elie de Beaumont. This learned man, well placed in the scientific world, held that the soil of Moulin-Quignon did not belong to the diluvium, but to a much later strata, and he would by no means admit that the human species was contemporary with the animals of the Quaternary epoch. Mr. Elie de Beaumont was pretty much alone in his opinions.

Other similar jawbones were found in France, Switzerland, and Belgium, and the probability of the existence of men in the Quaternary period became more positive every day.

It will now be easy to understand the professor's astonishment and joy when a few yards farther on he found himself face to face with a specimen of the human race actually belonging to the Quaternary period!

It was indeed a human body, perfectly recognizable. Had the peculiar nature of the soil here preserved it during countless ages? For this body, with stretched and parchmentlike skin, with the teeth whole, the hair abundant, was before our eyes as in life!

I stood mute with wonder and awe before this dread apparition of another age. My uncle, on every occasion a great talker, remained for a time completely dumbfounded. After a while, however, he raised up the body to which the skull belonged. We stood it on end. The figure seemed to our excited imaginations to look at us with its terrible hollow eyes.

After some minutes of silence Professor Hardwigg, carried away by his enthusiasm, forgot the extraordinary position in which we were placed and imagined himself at the Institute addressing his attentive pupils. He put on his most doctorial style, waved his hand, and began.

"Gentlemen, I have the honor to present to you a man of the Quaternary period of our globe. Many learned men have denied his very existence.

"But after what we now see, to doubt is to insult scientific inquiry. There is a body; you can see it; you can touch it. It is not a skeleton, it is a complete and uninjured body."

Here the professor held up the fossil body and exhibited it with rare dexterity. No professional showman could have done better.

"On examination you will see," my uncle continued, "it is only about six feet in length, which is a long way from being a giant.

"Yes, this is a fossil man, a contemporary of the mastodons. But if I am called on to explain how he came to this place, I can give you no explanation. Doubtless, if we carry ourselves back to the Quaternary period, we shall find that mighty convulsions took place in the crust of the earth. The continual cooling operation through which the earth had to pass produced fissures, landslips, and chasms through which a large portion of the earth made its way. I come to no absolute conclusion, but there is the man. The only rational explanation is that, like myself, he visited the center of the earth as a traveling tourist, a pioneer of science. There can be no doubt of his great age, and of his being one of the oldest of the race of human beings."

The professor with these words ceased his

oration, and I burst forth into loud and "unanimous" applause.

We soon discovered that that fossilized body was not the only one in this vast plain of bones. Other bodies were found, and my uncle was able to choose from them the most marvelous specimens, in order to convince the most incredulous.

It was a surprising spectacle, the successive remains of generation upon generation of men and animals together in one vast cemetery. But a great question now presented itself. One we were actually afraid to contemplate in all its effects.

Had these once animated beings lived here below in this subterranean world, under this artificial sky, been born, married, given in marriage, then dying at last, just like inhabitants of the earth?

Up to the present moment, only marine monsters, fish, and such like animals had we seen alive!

Were any of these men of the abyss wandering about the deserted shores of this wondrous sea in the center of the earth?

This was a question which made me very uneasy. If they existed, how would they receive us men from above?

What Is It?

For a long and weary hour we tramped over this great bed of bones, drawn on by curiosity. The borders of the Central Sea had some time ago disappeared behind the hills. The professor, who did not care whether he got lost or not, hurried forward. We advanced silently, bathed in waves of electric fluid.

By reason of a phenomenon which I cannot explain, the light illumined equally the sides of every hill and rock, and produced no shade whatever.

After we had walked about a mile farther, we came to the edge of a vast forest, not, however, one of the vast mushroom forests we had discovered near Port Gretchen.

This was the glorious and wild vegetation of the Tertiary period: huge palms, of a species now unknown, pines, yews, cypress, conifers, or cone-bearing trees — the whole bound together by a complicated mass of creeping plants.

A beautiful carpet of mosses and ferns grew beneath the trees. Pleasant brooks murmured beside small treelike shrubs.

The one thing lacking in these plants, shrubs, and trees was color! Forever deprived of the warmth of the sun, all were cloaked in one uniform tint of brown. The numerous flowers were without perfume.

My uncle ventured beneath the gigantic groves. I followed him, though full of apprehension.

Suddenly I stopped short and restrained my uncle. I saw with my own eyes gigantic animals moving about under the mighty trees. They were truly gigantic animals, a whole herd of mastodons, not fossils, but living, and exactly like those discovered in 1801 on the marshy banks of the great Ohio in North America.

I could see these enormous elephants, whose trunks were tearing down large boughs and working in and out of the trees like a legion of serpents. I could hear the sounds of the mighty tusks uprooting huge trees!

That wondrous dream, when I saw the Tertiary and Quaternary periods pass before me, was now realized!

And here we were alone, far down in the bowels of the earth, at the mercy of its ferocious inhabitants!

My uncle paused, full of wonder and astonishment.

"Come," he said at last. "Come, let us go nearer."

"No." I restrained his efforts to drag me forward. "Come away, Uncle, I beg you. No human creature can brave the anger of these monsters."

"No human creature," said my uncle, suddenly lowering his voice to a mysterious whisper. "You are mistaken, my dear Harry. Look! Yonder! A being like ourselves — a man!"

Not more than a quarter of a mile off, leaning against the trunk of an enormous tree, was a human being. The shepherd of the gigantic cattle, he was himself a giant!

It was no fossil corpse we had raised from the ground in the cemetery, but a giant. His height was above twelve feet. His head, as big as the head of a buffalo, was lost in a mane of matted hair. In his hand was a branch of a tree, which served as a crook to drive the cattle.

We remained perfectly still, speechless with surprise.

But we might at any moment be seen.

"Come, come!" I urged, dragging my uncle along. For the first time, he made no resistance.

A quarter of an hour later we were far away from that terrible monster!

Now that I can think of the matter calmly, now that months, years have passed since this strange and unnatural adventure, what do I think? What do I believe?

Our ears must have deceived us, and our eyes have cheated us! We could not have seen what we believed we had seen. No generation of men could inhabit the lower caverns of the globe. It was folly to think so, nothing else!

I am inclined to believe it was some animal resembling in structure the human — some monkey of the first geological epochs.

But this animal, this being, whichever it was, surpassed in height all things known to modern science. It might have been a monkey — but a man, a living man buried in the entrails of the earth — it was too monstrous to be believed!

The Mysterious Dagger

We were dumb with astonishment. We kept running in spite of ourselves. It was a horrible sensation, such as one sometimes meets in a dream.

Instinctively we made our way toward the Central Sea. Though I was aware that we were treading on ground quite new to us, certain formations of rock reminded me of those near Port Gretchen.

Then, as we advanced still farther, the position of the cliffs, the appearance of a stream, the unexpected profile of a rock threw me into a state of bewildering doubt.

I explained my puzzlement to my uncle and he confessed to a similar feeling. He was totally unable to make up his mind in the midst of this extraordinary but uniform panorama.

"There can be no doubt," I insisted, "that we have not landed at the exact place where we took our departure. But I think that if we follow the coast we shall once more find Port Gretchen."

"In that case," cried my uncle, "the best thing we can do is to make our way back to the raft. Are you quite sure, Harry, that you are not mistaken?"

"It is difficult to come to any firm decision. At the same time, I think I recognize the promontory at the foot of which Hans constructed the raft. I am convinced that we are near the port. If not at it," I said, examining a creek which appeared singularly familiar to me.

"My dear Harry, if this were the place, we should find traces of our own footsteps, some sign of our passage. I can see nothing to indicate our having passed this way."

"I see something," I cried. I rushed forward and eagerly picked up something which shone in the sand under my feet.

"What is it?" cried the professor.

"This," was my reply as I handed my startled relative a rusty dagger.

"What made you bring so useless a weapon with you?" my uncle explained.

"*I* bring it? I never saw it before. Are you sure it is not from your collection?"

"No," said the professor. "It was never my property. There is a very simple explanation, Harry. This must have belonged to Hans."

I shook my head. That dagger had never been in the possession of Hans. I knew him and his habits too well.

"It must be the weapon of some antediluvian warrior, some living man, a contemporary of that one from whom we have just escaped? But no! Mystery upon mystery! This is no weapon of the Stone Age, nor even of the Bronze Age. It is made of excellent steel — "

My uncle stopped me short. "Calm yourself, my dear boy, and endeavor to use your reason. This weapon is a true *dague*, one of those worn by gentlemen in the sixteenth century. Its use was to give the *coup de grace*, the final blow, to the foe who would not surrender. It is clearly of Spanish workmanship. It belongs neither to you, nor to me, nor to Hans — nor to any living beings who may still exist in the interior of the earth."

"What can you mean, Uncle?" I said.

"Look closely at it," he continued. "These jagged edges were never made by the resistance of human blood and bone. The blade is covered with a regular coating of iron mold and rust, which is not a day old, not a year old, not a century old — but much more."

The professor began to get quite excited, as was his custom.

"Harry," he cried, "we are on the verge of a great discovery. This dagger you so marvelously discovered has been chipped by someone endeavoring to carve an inscription on these rocks."

"Someone, therefore, must have preceded us on the shores of this extraordinary sea."

"Yes, a man."

"But what man?"

"A man who has somewhere written his name with this very dagger — a man who endeavored once more to indicate the right road to the interior of the earth. Let us look around, my boy. You know not the importance of your discovery."

We walked along the wall of rock, examining the smallest fissure which might expand into the much wished for gully or shaft.

We at last reached a spot where the shore became extremely narrow. The sea almost bathed the foot of the rocks. At last, under a huge overhanging rock, we discovered the entrance of a dark and gloomy tunnel.

There, on a square tablet of granite which had been smoothed by rubbing it with another stone, we could see two letters, the initials of the extraordinary traveler who had preceded us on our adventurous journey.

"A.S." cried my uncle. "You see I was right. Arne Saknussemm, always Arne Saknussemm!"

No Outlet—Blasting the Rock

Ever since the start of our journey, I had experienced many surprises. I thought that I was hardened and could neither see nor hear anything to amaze me again.

When, however, I saw these two letters, which had been engraved three hundred years before, I stood fixed in an attitude of mute surprise.

Not only was the signature of the learned and enterprising alchemist written in the rock, but I held in my hand the very instrument with which he had laboriously engraved it.

It was impossible to deny the existence of the traveler and the reality of that voyage which I believed all along to have been a myth.

My uncle gave way to an excess of poetical excitement.

"Wonderful and glorious genius! Great Saknussemm!" he cried. "The traveler who follows your footsteps to the last will doubtless find your initials engraved with your own hand upon the center of the earth. I will be that audacious traveler. I, too, will sign my name upon the very same spot, upon the central granite stone of this wondrous work of the creator. But in justice to your devotion, to your courage, and to your being the first to indicate the road, let this cape be called for all time, Cape Saknussemm."

A fierce excitement aroused me. I forgot the dangers of the voyage, and the perils of the return journey were now as nothing. What another man had done in ages past, I felt could be done again. I was determined to do it myself, and now nothing that man had accomplished appeared to me impossible.

I had already started in the direction of the gloomy gallery when the professor stopped me.

"Let us return to Hans," he said. "We will then bring our raft down to this place."

I at once yielded to my uncle's request.

"Do you know, Uncle," I said, as we walked along, "that we have been helped by circumstances right up to this very moment."

"So you begin to see it, do you, Harry?" said the professor with a smile.

"Even the tempest has been the means of putting us on the right road," I said. "Suppose we had reached the opposite shore of this extraordinary sea, what would have become of us? We would never have found the initials of Saknussemm."

"Yes, Harry my boy, there was certainly something providential in our wandering. We have come back exactly north. And what is better still, we fall upon this great discovery of Cape Saknussemm. The coincidence is unheard of, marvelous!"

"Excuse me, sir, but I see exactly how it will be. We shall take the northern route. We shall pass under the northern regions of Europe, under Sweden, under Russia and Siberia, instead of burying ourselves under the burning plains and deserts of Africa and the mighty waves of the ocean."

"Yes, Harry, all is for the best. We shall descend, descend, and everlastingly descend. Do you know, my boy, that to reach the interior of the earth we have only five thousand miles to travel!"

"The distance is scarcely worth speaking about," I cried, quite carried away. "Let us make a start."

My wild speeches continued until we rejoined our patient guide. All was ready for an immediate departure. We took up our posts on the raft, and the sail being hoisted, Hans received his directions and guided the frail bark toward Cape Saknussemm.

The wind was very unfavorable for a craft that was unable to sail close to the wind. We had continually to push ourselves forward by means of poles. In some places the rocks ran far out into deep water, and we were forced to make long detours. At last, about six o'clock in the evening, we found a place at which we could land.

I jumped on shore first. My uncle and the Icelander followed. The voyage had by no means calmed me. Rather it had produced the opposite effect. I even began to think my uncle seemed unenthusiastic.

"My dear uncle," I said, "let us start without delay."

"My boy, I am quite as eager to start as you are. But first let us examine this mysterious gallery to see if we shall need our ladders."

The opening into the new gallery was not twenty paces distant from the landing spot. Myself at the head, we advanced.

The opening was almost circular, with a diameter of about five feet. The tunnel was cut in the living rock, and coated on the inside by the different material which had once passed through it in a state of fusion. The lower part was about level with the water.

We followed an almost horizontal direction. At the end of about a dozen paces, our advance was checked by an enormous block of granite rock.

I experienced the most bitter disappointment. Hans, with the Ruhmkorf's lamp, examined the sides of the tunnel in every direction. But all in vain! It was impossible to pass.

I had seated myself on the ground. My uncle walked angrily up and down. He was desperate.

"But what about Arne Saknussemm?" I cried.

"You are right," replied my uncle. "He would never have been stopped by a lump of rock."

"This huge rock has closed up the passage," I said. "This is an obstacle which Saknussemm did not meet. If we cannot move it in some way, we are unworthy of following in his footsteps — and incapable of finding our way to the center of the earth!"

In this wild way I addressed my uncle. His zeal, his earnest longing for success had become part and parcel of my being. I completely forgot the past. Nothing existed for me any longer on the surface of this spheroid — not Hamburg, the Konigstrasse, not even my poor Gretchen, who by this time must believe me utterly lost in the interior of the earth!

"Well," cried my uncle, roused to enthusiasm by my words, "let us go to work with pickaxes, with crowbars, with anything that comes to hand."

"It is far too big to be destroyed by a pickaxe or crowbar," I replied.

"What then?"

"What else but gunpowder?"

"Gunpowder!"

"Yes. We have to get rid of this obstacle."

"To work, Hans, to work!" cried the professor.

The Icelander went back to the raft and soon returned with a huge crowbar. He began to dig a hole, which was to serve as a mine, in the rock. It was no easy task. It was necessary to make a cavity large enough to hold fifty pounds of fulminating guncotton, the explosive power of which is four times as great as that of ordinary gunpowder.

While Hans was at work, I helped my uncle prepare a long wick, made from damp gunpowder. The mass of this we finally enclosed in a bag of linen.

At midnight our work was finished. The charge of fulminating cotton was placed in the hollow, and the wick, which we had made of considerable length, was ready.

A spark was all that was needed now to ignite this formidable force and to blow the rock to atoms!

"We will now rest until tomorrow," my uncle said.

I had to resign myself to waiting for six weary hours for the explosion!

The Explosion and Its Results

The next day, the twenty-ninth of August, was a celebrated date in our wondrous journey. I shudder with horror at the very memory of that awful day.

At six o'clock we were all up, and ready to seek an opening into the interior of the earth with gunpowder. What would be the consequence if we broke through the crust of the earth?

I begged that I might be the one to set fire to the charge. I looked upon it as an honor. I could then rejoin my friends on the raft, and we would sail away some distance to avoid the consequences of the explosion, which would certainly not be concentrated in the interior of the earth.

We calculated it would take about ten minutes for the slow fuse to reach the powder. I should therefore have plenty of time to reach the raft.

After a hearty meal, my uncle and Hans stood by with the raft, while I remained on shore.

I was provided with a lantern which would enable me to set fire to the wick.

"Go, my boy," said my uncle, "and be quick as you can."

I advanced toward the opening of the gallery. My heart beat wildly. I opened my lantern and seized the end of the wick.

The professor, who was looking on from the raft, held his chronometer in his hand.

"Are you ready?" he shouted.

"Quite ready."

"Fire away!"

I hastened to put the light to the wick, which crackled and sparkled, hissed and spit like a serpent. Then, running as fast as I could, I returned to the shore.

"Get on board, my lad. And you, Hans, shove off," cried my uncle.

Hans sent us flying over the water. In no time, the raft was quite twenty fathoms from the shore.

It was a moment of deep anxiety. My uncle never took his eyes off the chronometer.

"Only five minutes more," he said in a low tone. "Only four . . . only three . . ."

My pulse beat a hundred to the minute. I could hear my heart pounding.

"Only two . . . one . . ."

What happened after that? As for the roar of the explosion, I do not think I heard it. But the rocks seemed to be drawn aside like a curtain and I saw a fathomless, a bottomless abyss open beneath the turgid waves. The sea, which seemed suddenly to have gone mad, became one great mountainous mass on which the raft rose straight up.

We were all knocked down. In less than a second the light gave place to the most profound darkness. Then I felt all solid support give way — not to my feet but to the raft itself. I thought it was going bodily down a tremendous well. Nothing could be heard but the roaring of the waves. We clung together in utter silence.

Despite the awful darkness, despite the noise, the surprise, the emotion, I understood what had happened.

Beyond the rock which had been blown up, there existed a mighty abyss. The explosion had caused a kind of earthquake, causing fissures and rents in the ground. The gulf, thus suddenly thrown open, was about to swallow the inland sea which, transformed into a mighty torrent, was dragging us with it.

Only one idea filled my mind. We were utterly and completely doomed!

Hours passed. We sat close together, elbow touching elbow, knee touching knee! We held one another's hands not to be thrown off the raft. We were subjected to the most violent shocks whenever the raft struck against the rocky sides of the channel.

Finally these concussions became less frequent; evidently the gallery was getting wider. There could be now no doubt that we had chanced upon the road once followed by Saknussemm, but instead of going down in a proper manner, we had drawn a whole sea with us!

I sensed all this rather than reasoned it while I was spinning along like a man going down a waterfall. To judge by the air which whipped my face, we must have been rushing at a lightning rate. I was suddenly confused to see a bright light shining close to me. The calm countenance of Hans seemed to gleam upon me. The clever guide had succeeded in lighting the lantern. Though the flame flickered and was nearly put out, it served partially to dissipate the awful darkness.

The gallery which we had entered was very wide. The rush of water carrying us away was far stronger than the most rapid river in America. The raft at times caught in whirlpools, then rushed forward. Why it did not upset I shall never be able to understand. So rapid was our progress that sharp points of rock at considerable distance from one another appeared to run together like the lines of telegraph wires.

I believe we were now going at a rate of not less than a hundred miles an hour.

My uncle and I looked at one another with haggard eyes. We clung to the stump of the mast which, at the moment when the catastrophe took place, had snapped off short. We turned our backs as much as possible to the wind, which no human could face and live.

When we had slightly recovered our equilibrium, I examined our cargo. The greater part of it had utterly disappeared.

Of our collection of instruments there remained only the chronometer and the compass — not a pickaxe, not a crowbar, not a hammer. Far worse, no food — not enough for one day!

Our stock of provisions consisted of a piece of dry meat and some soaked biscuits.

I gazed around me, frightened. I could not believe the awful truth. And yet of what consequence was it? Supposing we had provisions for months, even for years, how could we ever get out of the awful abyss into which we were being hurled by the torrent we had let loose?

It was very doubtful, under the circumstances, whether we should have time to die of starvation. But, after all, we might possibly escape the fury of the raging torrent and once more see the moon on the surface of our beautiful earth. How? I had not the remotest idea. Where were we to come out? No matter, just so we did.

One chance in a thousand is always a chance. While death from hunger gave not even the faintest glimpse of hope.

At this moment, the light of the lantern slowly dimmed and at last went out. It was no longer possible to see through the impenetrable darkness! There was one torch left, but it was impossible to keep it alight. Then, like a child, I shut my eyes so that I might not see the darkness.

After a great lapse of time, the speed of our journey increased. I could feel it by the rush of air upon my face. The slope of the waters was excessive. I began to feel that we were no longer going down a slope, but that we were falling. I felt as one does in a dream — falling, falling, falling.

Then very quickly I felt something like a shock; the raft had not struck a hard body but had suddenly been checked in its course. A waterspout, a liquid column of water, fell upon us. I felt suffocated. I was being drowned. But this sudden inundation did not last. In a few seconds I felt myself once more able to breathe. My uncle and Hans locked arms with me, and the raft still bore us onward.

The Ape Gigans

It is difficult for me to determine what time it was, but I should suppose, after calculating, that it must have been ten at night.

I lay in a stupor, a half dream. The raft took a sudden turn, whirled around, and entered another tunnel lit in a most singular manner. The roof was formed of porous stalactites, through which a moonlit vapor appeared to pass. The light increased as we advanced. We were once more in a kind of watery cavern, the lofty dome of which disappeared in a luminous cloud.

And now a small dry cavern appeared that offered a halting place to our weary bodies. It seemed to me that we were moving like men in a dream. Somehow we had left the raft and now I was seated near my companions to keep watch.

Suddenly I became aware of something moving in the distance. It was floating, apparently upon the surface of the water, advancing by means of what at first appeared paddles. One glance told me that it was something monstrous.

But what?

It was the great shark-crocodile about which the early geologists wrote. About the size of an ordinary whale, with hideous jaws and two gigantic eyes, it advanced, its eyes fixed on me. Some indefinite warning told me that it had marked me for its own.

I attempted to rise, to escape — no matter where — but my knees shook under me, my limbs trembled violently, and still the mighty monster advanced. My uncle and Hans did not stir to save themselves.

With a strange noise, like none I had ever heard before, the beast came on. His jaws were at least seven feet apart, his distended mouth looked large enough to have swallowed a boatful of men.

His body resembled that of a crocodile and his mouth was wholly that of a shark.

With a wild cry, I darted away into the interior of the cavern, leaving my unhappy comrades to their fate! After about a hundred yards I paused and looked around.

The whole floor, composed of sand and malachite, was strewn with bones — freshly gnawed bones of reptiles and fish. I grew sick with horror. Some beast larger and more ferocious even than the shark-crocodile must inhabit this den.

What could I do? The mouth of the cave was guarded by one ferocious monster, the interior was inhabited by something too hideous to contemplate. Flight was impossible!

I gazed around wildly, and at last discovered a crevice in the rock to which I rushed to hide myself. Crouching down, I waited, shivering as in a fever.

An hour passed. All the time I heard a strange rumbling outside the cave.

Suddenly a groaning, like the sound of fifty bears in a fight, fell upon my ears — hisses, spitting, moaning, hideous to hear. And then I saw —

Never shall I forget the horrible apparition.

It was the Ape Gigans, the antediluvian gorilla.

Fourteen feet high, covered with coarse hair of a blackish brown, it advanced. Its arms were as long as its body, and its legs were huge. It had thick, long, sharply pointed teeth — like a mammoth saw.

It struck its breast as it came on, smelling and sniffing, reminding me of the stories I had read in childhood of giants who ate the flesh of men and women!

Suddenly it stopped. My heart beat wildly, for I was conscious that somehow or other the fearful monster had smelt me out and was peering about with his hideous eyes to try and discover my whereabouts.

At this moment there came a strange noise from the entrance of the cave. Turning, the gorilla evidently recognized some enemy more worthy of his size and strength. It was the huge shark-crocodile which, perhaps, having disposed of my friends, was coming in search of further prey.

The gorilla placed himself on the defensive, and clutching a bone some seven or eight feet in length, a perfect club, aimed a deadly blow at the hideous beast. The shark crocodile reared upwards and fell with all its weight upon its adversary.

A terrible combat now ensued. The struggle was awful. I slid down from my hiding place, reached the ground, and gliding against the wall, tried to gain the open mouth of the cavern.

But I had not taken many steps when the fearful clamor ceased, to be followed by a mumbling and groaning which appeared to be indicative of victory.

I looked back and saw the huge ape, gory with blood, coming after me with glaring eyes, and with dilated nostrils that gave forth two columns of heated vapor. I could feel his hot and fetid breath on my neck, and with a horrid jump I awoke from my nightmare sleep.

Yes — it was all a dream. I was still on the raft with my uncle and Hans.

Relief was instantaneous, but all was still as death. The roaring I had imagined filling the gallery with awful reverberations was succeeded by perfect peace.

My uncle spoke in a scarcely audible tone.

"Harry, boy, where are you?"

"I am here," was my faint rejoinder.

"Do you see what is happening? We are going upwards."

"What can you mean?" was my half-delirious reply.

"Yes, I tell you we are ascending rapidly."

I held out my hand and after some difficulty succeeded in touching the wall. In an instant my hand was covered with blood. The skin was torn from the flesh. We were ascending with extraordinary speed.

"The torch — the torch!" said the professor wildly. "It must be lighted."

Hans, after many vain efforts, succeeded in lighting it. The flame shed a tolerably clear light.

"It is just as I thought," said my uncle, after a moment or two of silent examination. "We are in a narrow well about four fathoms square. The waters of the great inland sea, having reached the bottom of the gulf, are now forcing themselves up the mighty shaft. As a natural consequence, we are being cast up on the summit of the waters."

"I can see that," I said. "But where will this shaft end, and to what are we likely to be exposed next?"

"All I know is that we should be prepared for the worst. We are going up at a fearfully rapid rate — two fathoms a second, or a hundred and twenty fathoms a minute. At this rate our fate will soon be a certainty."

"No doubt of it," was my reply. "But I am concerned about whether this shaft has any opening or whether it ends in a granite roof — in which case we shall be suffocated by compressed air or dashed to atoms against the top."

"Harry," said the professor, "the situation is desperate but there is a chance. We may at any moment perish, or at any moment we may be saved! We must prepare ourselves for whatever may turn up."

"But what would you have us do?" I cried.

"While there is life there is hope. There is one thing we can do — eat and obtain strength to face victory or death."

As he spoke, I knew I must tell him the truth.

Turning around to the guide, my uncle spoke some cheering words in Danish. Hans shook his head.

"What!" cried the professor. "Do you mean to say that all our provisions are lost?"

"Yes," I replied, as I held out my hand. "This morsel of dried meat is all that remains for us three."

My uncle gazed at me. The blow seemed to stun him.

"Well," I said. "What do you think now? Are we not doomed to perish in the great hollows of the center of the earth?"

My question brought no answer. I began

to feel the most fearful and devouring hunger. My companions, doubtless, felt the same, but neither of them would touch the morsel of meat that remained. It lay there, a last remnant of all our great preparations for this mad and senseless journey!

The Last Meal

Hunger prolonged leads to temporary madness! The brain is at work without its required food, and fantastic notions fill the mind. I had never known what hunger really meant. I was likely to find out now.

After dreaming for some time, and thinking on hunger and other matters, I once more looked around me. We were still rising with fearful speed. The heat began to increase in a most threatening manner. I cannot tell exactly, but I think it must have reached 50° Centigrade (122° F.).

What was the meaning of this extraordinary change in the temperature? Until now the peculiar qualities of refractory rocks had created a moderate temperature for us inside the earth.

But the theory of the central fire remained, in my eyes, the only explainable one. Were we going to reach a position in which the heat would reduce the rocks to a state of fusion?

Such was my fear and I did not conceal the fact from my uncle. My way of doing so might be thought cold and heartless, but I could not help it.

"If we are not drowned or smashed into pancakes, and if we do not die of starvation, dear Uncle, we have the satisfaction of knowing that we will be burned alive."

My uncle, in answer to this brusque attack, simply shrugged his shoulders.

An hour passed with a slight increase in temperature.

At last, my uncle broke his silence.

"Well, Harry, my boy," he said, in a cheerful voice, "we must make up our minds."

"To what?" I asked.

"Well, we must keep up our physical strength. If we make the mistake of rationing our little remnant of food, we may probably prolong our wretched existence a few hours — but we shall remain weak all the time."

"When this piece of meat is gone, Uncle, what hope will there be for us?"

"None, my dear Harry, none. But will it do you any good to devour it with your eyes?

You appear to me to reason like one without will or decision, like a being without energy."

"Do you mean to tell me," I cried, exasperated, "that you have not lost all hope?"

"Certainly not," replied the professor, with consummate coolness.

"You really believe, Uncle, that we shall get out of this monstrous subterranean shaft?"

"Harry, I do not understand how a being like you, gifted with thought and will, can allow himself to despair."

"Well," I cried, "what do you plan to do?"

"Eat what remains of the food. It will be our last meal."

"True," I muttered in a despairing tone, "let us take our fill."

My uncle took the piece of meat and some crusts of biscuit which had escaped the wreck. He divided it all into three parts.

Each of us had one pound of food to last him as long as he remained in the interior of the earth.

My uncle ate greedily, but without appetite. I put the food inside my lips and, hungry as I was, chewed my morsel without pleasure and without satisfaction.

Hans swallowed every mouthful, as though it were nothing unusual. His hardy Icelandic nature had prepared him for many sufferings.

Suddenly my uncle roused himself. He had seen a smile on the face of our guide.

"What is it?" said my uncle.

"Schiedem," said the guide, producing a bottle of this precious liquid.

We drank. My uncle and myself will own, to our dying day, that from it we derived strength to exist until the last bitter moment.

"Fortrafflig," said Hans, swallowing nearly all that was left.

"Excellent — very good," said my uncle, with as much gusto as if he had just left his club in Hamburg.

And so we consumed our last meal together. It was five o'clock in the morning!

The Volcanic Shaft

No sooner is the rage of hunger appeased, than it becomes difficult to comprehend the meaning of starvation. It is only when you suffer that you really understand.

Some mouthfuls of bread and meat, a little moldy biscuit and salt beef triumphed over all our previous gloomy thoughts.

Nevertheless, after this meal each gave way to his own reflections. My thoughts were all connected with that upper world which I never should have left. I saw it all — the beautiful house in the Konigstrasse, my poor Gretchen, Martha our cook — all passed before my mind like visions of the past.

My uncle, always thinking of his science, examined the shaft by means of the torch. I heard him, as I sat in silence, murmuring words of geological science. As I understood his object, I could not help being interested.

"Eruptive granite," he said to himself. "We are still in the primitive epoch. We are going up. But who knows —"

Then he still hoped. Some few minutes later he went on again.

"This is gneiss. This is mocashites — siliceous mineral. Good. This is the epoch of transition, at all events, we are close to them — and then, and then — "

What could he mean? Could he, by any means, measure the thickness of the crust of the earth suspended about our heads? No. The manometer was missing and no summary calculation could take the place of it.

And yet, as we progressed, the temperature increased to a most extraordinary degree. I began to feel as if I were bathed in a hot and burning atmosphere. Never before had I felt anything like it. By degrees Hans, my uncle, and myself had taken off our coats and waistcoats. They were unbearable. Even the slightest garment was not only uncomfortable but the cause of extreme suffering.

"Are we ascending to a living fire?" I cried, when the heat became even greater.

"No, no," said my uncle. "It is simply impossible, quite impossible."

"And yet," I said, touching the side of the shaft with my hand, "this wall is literally burning."

I plunged my hands into the water to cool them, but I drew them back with a cry of despair.

"The water is boiling!" I cried.

My uncle made no reply other than a gesture of rage and despair.

Something very like the truth had probably struck him.

An invincible dread took possession of me. I could only look forward to an immediate catastrophe.

I tremulously rejected it at first, but it forced itself upon me by degrees. It was so terrible an idea that I scarcely dared to whisper it to myself.

And yet all the while certain involuntary observations determined my convictions. By the doubtful glare of the torch, I could make out some changes in the granitic strata. A strange and terrible phenomenon was about to be produced in which electricity played a part. I determined as a last resource to examine the compass.

The compass had gone mad!

The needle jumped from pole to pole with sudden and surprising jerks, ran around, boxed the compass, and then ran suddenly back again as if it had vertigo.

I was aware that, according to the best acknowledged theories, the mineral crust of the globe is never, and was never, in a state of complete rest. Human beings on its surface do not suspect the seething process going on.

Still this phenomenon alone would not have aroused in my mind such a terrible, awful idea, if other facts had not presented themselves.

We heard terrible detonations that multiplied with fearful intensity. I could only compare the sound to a continuous roll of heavy thunder.

And then the mad compass, shaken by the wild electric phenomena, confirmed me in my rapidly forming opinion. The mineral crust was about to burst, heavy granite masses were about to merge, the fissure was about to close, the void was about to be filled up, and we poor atoms to be crushed in its awful embrace!

"Uncle, Uncle!" I cried. "We are wholly, irretrievably lost!"

"What is your new cause of terror and alarm?" he said, in his calmest manner. "What do you fear now?"

"What do I fear now!" I cried fiercely. "Do you not see that the walls of the shaft are in motion? Do you not see that the solid granite masses are cracking? Do you not

266

feel the terrible, torrid heat? Do you not observe the awful boiling water on which we float? Do you not see this mad needle? Here is every sign and portent of an awful earthquake!"

My uncle coolly shook his head.

"No earthquake," he replied, in the most calm and provoking tone.

"*Yes.*"

"Nephew, I tell you that you are mistaken," he continued.

"Do you not — can you not — recognize all the well-known signs?"

"Of an earthquake? By no means. I am expecting something far more important."

"What? What do you mean?" I cried.

"An eruption, Harry."

"An eruption," I gasped. "We are then in the volcanic shaft of a crater in full action and vigor?"

"I have every reason to think so," said the professor in a smiling tone. "And I beg to tell you that it is the most fortunate thing that could happen to us."

The most fortunate thing! Had my uncle really and truly gone mad? What did he mean by these awful words? What did he mean by his terrible calm, his solemn smile?

"We are on the way to an eruption, are

we?" I cried, in the height of exasperation. "Fate has cast us into a well of burning and boiling lava. We are about to be expelled, thrown up, vomited, spit out of the interior of the earth in a wild whirlwind of flame, and you say it is the most fortunate thing which could happen to us."

"Yes," replied the professor, looking at me calmly from under his spectacles. "It is the only chance which remains to us of ever escaping from the interior of the earth to the light of day."

It is quite impossible to put on paper the thousand strange, wild thoughts which came to me following this extraordinary announcement.

But my uncle was right, and never had he appeared to me so audacious and so certain as when he looked me in the face and spoke of the chances of an eruption — of our being cast upon the earth through the gaping crater of a volcano!

While we were speaking we were still ascending. We passed the whole night going up. The fearful noise redoubled. I believed that my last hour was approaching.

It was quite evident that we were being cast upwards by eruptive matter. Under the raft there was a mass of boiling water, and under this was a heaving mass of lava and rocks, which on reaching the summit of the water would be dispersed in every direction.

There could no longer be the shadow of a doubt that we were inside the chimney of a volcano.

But instead of being inside Sneffels, an old and extinct volcano, we were inside a mountain of fire in full activity. Several times I found myself asking what mountain it was and on what part of the world we should be shot out. As if it were of any consequence!

Before it went mad the compass had never made the slightest mistake. Now the question was, were we once more under Iceland — should we be belched forth onto the earth through the crater of Mount Hecla? Or should we reappear through one of the other seven fire funnels of the island? Taking into account a radius of five hundred leagues to the westward, we could come up through one of the little-known volcanoes of the northwest coast of America.

To the east, only one existed — the Esk on the island of Jean Mayen, not far from the frozen regions of Spitzbergen.

It was not that craters were lacking. All I wished to know was the particular one toward which we were making with such fearful velocity.

Toward morning the ascending motion became greater and greater. An enormous force, a force of some hundreds of combined atmospheres long compressed in the interior of the earth, were hoisting us upwards with irresistible power.

But though we were approaching the light of day, to what fearful dangers were we about to be exposed?

Instant death appeared the only fate which we could expect or contemplate.

Soon a dim, sepulchral light penetrated the vertical gallery, which became wider and wider. I could make out to the right and left long dark corridors, like immense tunnels, from which awful and horrid vapors poured out. Tongues of fire, sparkling and crackling, appeared about to lick us up.

The hour had come!

"Look, Uncle, look!" I cried.

"What you see are the great sulphurous flames that come with an eruption."

"But if they lap around us!" I angrily replied.

"They will not lap around us," was his quiet and serene answer.

"It will be all the same in the end if they stifle us," I cried.

"We shall not be stifled. The gallery is becoming wider and wider. If it becomes necessary, we will leave the raft and take refuge in some fissure in the rock."

"But the water, the water which is continually ascending?" I despairingly replied.

"There is no longer any water, Harry," he answered, "but a kind of lava paste that is heaving us up to the mouth of the crater."

In truth, the liquid column of water had disappeared to give place to dense masses of boiling eruptive matter. The temperature was becoming insupportable. Perspiration rushed from every pore. But for the extraordinary speed of our ascent we should have been stifled.

Nevertheless the professor did not follow his proposal to abandon the raft, and he was wise. Those few ill-joined beams offered a solid surface, a support which elsewhere might have utterly failed us.

Toward eight o'clock in the morning a new incident startled us. The upward movement suddenly ceased. The raft became still and motionless.

"What is the matter now?" I said, startled by this change.

"A simple halt," replied my uncle.

"Is the eruption about to fail?" I asked.

"I hope not."

Without making any reply, I rose. I tried to look around me. Perhaps the raft had been checked by some projecting rock.

Nothing of the kind had occurred. The column of cinders, scoriae, broken rocks, and earth had wholly ceased to ascend.

"I tell you, Uncle, that the eruption has stopped."

"You are wrong, my boy. This sudden moment of calm will not last long, be assured. It has already lasted five minutes, and before many more minutes we shall be continuing our journey to the mouth of the crater."

All the time he was speaking the professor continued to consult his chronometer. Soon the raft resumed its motion in a rapid and disorderly way. This lasted two minutes or thereabouts, and then it stopped as suddenly as before.

"Good," said my uncle. "In ten minutes we shall start again."

"In ten minutes?"

"Yes — precisely. The eruption of a volcano is intermittent. We are compelled to move just as it does."

Nothing could be more true. At the exact minute he had indicated, we were again launched on high. Then the hoist again ceased. It appeared quite clear to me that we were not in the principal chimney of the volcano but in an accessory conduit, where we felt the countershock of the great and principal tunnel.

It is impossible for me to say how many times this hoisting maneuver was repeated. All that I can remember is that we were hoisted up with ever-increasing velocity, as if we had been launched from a huge projectile. During the halts we were nearly stifled; during the moments of projection the hot air took away our breath.

By degrees my head, utterly overcome by a series of violent emotions, began to give way to hallucination. I was delirious. Had it not been for Hans, I should have cracked my head against the granite sides of the shaft.

I have, in consequence, no recollection of what followed for many hours. I have a vague and confused remembrance of continual detonations, of the shaking of the huge granitic mass, and of the raft going around like a spinning top. It floated on the stream of hot lava, amidst a falling cloud of cinders. The huge flames, roaring, wrapped around us.

A storm of wind which appeared to be cast forth from an immense ventilator roused up the interior fires of the earth. It was a hot incandescent blast.

I saw the figure of Hans as if enveloped in a huge halo of burning fire. No other sense remained to me but the sinister dread which the condemned victim may be supposed to feel when the shot is fired and his limbs are dispersed into empty space.

Daylight at Last

W hen I opened my eyes I felt the hand of the guide clutching me firmly by the belt. With his other hand he supported my uncle. I was not badly hurt, but bruised and seared all over in the most remarkable manner.

After a moment I looked around, and found that I was lying on the slope of a mountain not two yards from a yawning gulf into which I should have fallen had I made the slightest false step. Hans had saved me from death.

"Where are we?" asked my uncle, who appeared to be disgusted at having returned to earth.

Hans simply shrugged his shoulders.

"In Iceland?" I said, not positively but interrogatively.

"*Nej,*" said Hans.

"How do you know?" cried the professor. "What are you reasons?"

"Hans is wrong," I said, expecting to see a cone covered by snow, and the extensive glaciers of the extreme northern regions.

But contrary to all my expectations, we had been cast up on a mountain heated by the burning rays of a sun which was literally baking us with its heat.

I could not believe my eyes, but the heat which affected my body left me little chance to doubt. We came out of the crater half naked, and the sun from which we had asked nothing for two months was good enough to offer us light and warmth.

After some delay, the professor spoke.

"Hem!" he said, in a hesitating kind of way. "It really does not look like Iceland."

"It might be the island of Jean Mayen?" I ventured to observe.

"No, my boy. This is not one of the volcanoes of the north, with its hills of granite and its crown of snow."

"Nevertheless — "

"Look, look, my boy," said the professor.

Right above our heads opened the crater of a volcano from which escaped a lofty jet of flame mingled with pumice stone, cinders, and lava. I could feel the convulsions of nature in the mountain, which breathed like a huge whale, throwing up fire and air through its enormous vents.

Below me the stream of eruptive matter spread away to a great depth. The base of the volcano disappeared in a perfect forest of green trees, among which I could see olives, fig trees, and vines loaded with rich grapes.

Certainly this was not the arctic regions. Beyond the verdant expanse lay the waters of a lovely sea or beautiful lake which made an island of this enchanted land.

On one side of the island was a little port, crowded with houses. Boats and vessels of unfamiliar shapes were floating on the azure waves.

Toward the setting sun we made out some distant shore on the edge of the horizon. Toward the north lay an immense expanse of water, sparkling beneath the sun's rays. Occasionally we saw the top of a mast, or a sail bellying to the wind.

"Where can we be?" I asked.

"Wherever this mountain may be," my uncle said at last. "I must confess it is rather warm. Let us carefully descend the mountain and find out. To tell the truth, I am dying of hunger and thirst."

The slope of the volcano was very steep

and slippery. We slid over piles of ashes, avoiding streams of hot lava which glided about like fiery serpents. I spoke continually.

"We are in Asia!" I exclaimed. "We are on the coast of India, on the great Malay islands, in the center of Oceania. We have crossed one half of the globe to come out right at the antipodes of Europe!"

"But the compass!" exclaimed my uncle. "Explain that to me!"

"Yes — the compass," I said. "I grant that is a difficulty. According to it, we have always been going north."

"Then it lied."

"To say it lied is rather a harsh word," was my answer.

"Then we are at the North Pole."

"The Pole, no. I give up," was my reply.

The plain truth was that there was no explanation I could make.

After two long hours march, a beautiful country spread out before us, covered with olives, pomegranates, and vines, which appeared to belong to anybody and everybody.

What delight it was to bite into the grapes and pomegranates fresh from the vine. Not far off, near some fresh and mossy grass, I discovered a spring of fresh water in which we bathed our burning faces, hands, and feet.

While we were giving way to the delights of these new found pleasures, a young boy appeared between two tufted olive trees.

The little fellow was poorly dressed and appeared alarmed at our appearance. Half naked, with tangled, matted, and ragged beards, we did look rather ill-favored.

Just as the boy was about to take to his heels, Hans ran after him and brought him back despite his cries and kicks.

My uncle tried to look as gentle as possible, and then spoke in German.

"What is the name of this mountain, my friend?"

The child made no reply.

"Good," said my uncle. "We are not in Germany."

He then made the same demand in English.

The child shook his head and made no reply. I began to be considerably puzzled.

"Is he deaf?" cried the professor after making the same demand in French. My uncle was rather proud of his knowledge of languages.

The boy only stared in his face.

"I'll try him in Italian," said my uncle, with a shrug.

"Dove noi siamo?"

"Tell me where we are?" I said, impatiently.

Still the boy remained silent.

"My fine fellow, do you or do you not mean to speak?" cried my uncle, who had begun to get angry. He shook the boy and spoke to him again in another dialect of the Italian language.

Come si noma questa isola?" ("What is the name of this island?")

"Stromboli," replied the rickety little shepherd, before dashing away from Hans and disappearing in the olive groves.

Stromboli! We were in the center of the Mediterranean. Those blue mountains which rose toward the sun were the mountains of Calabria.

And that mighty volcano which rose on the southern horizon was Etna. The fierce and celebrated Etna!

"Stromboli!" I repeated to myself.

Ah — what a journey — what a marvelous and extraordinary journey! We had entered the earth by one volcano, and we had come out by another. And this other was more than twelve hundred leagues from Sneffels, from that dreary country of Iceland.

We had abandoned the region of eternal

snows for that of infinite verdure. We had left the gray fog of the icy regions and come back to the azure sky of Italy!

After a delicious meal of fruits and fresh water, we again continued our journey to the port we had seen from the top of the volcano. We decided it was safer to pass for humble and unfortunate shipwrecked travelers.

As we walked, I could hear my uncle muttering to himself.

"But the compass. The compass most certainly pointed north. This is a fact I cannot explain in any way."

"The fact is," I said, "we must not explain anything. It will be much easier."

"I should like to meet a professor of the Johanneum Institute who is unable to explain a cosmic phenomenon — it would indeed be strange."

Speaking thus, my uncle became once more the terrible professor of mineralogy.

An hour later we reached the Port of San Vicenza, where Hans demanded the price of his thirteenth week of service. My uncle paid him, with a very warm handshake.

With the tips of two fingers Hans gently pressed our hands and smiled.

The Journey Ended

This is the conclusion of a narrative which will probably be disbelieved, even by people who are astonished at nothing. I am, however, armed at all points against human incredulity.

We were kindly received by the Stromboli fishermen who treated us as shipwrecked travelers. They gave us clothes and food. After a delay of forty-eight hours, on the thirty-first of September a small boat took us to Messina, where a few days of complete rest restored us.

On the fourth of October we embarked on the *Volturus*, one of the postal packets of the Imperial Messagerie of France. Three days later we landed at Marseilles, with no other care on our minds than our erratic compass. This inexplicable circumstance tormented me. On the ninth of October, in the evening, we reached Hamburg.

What was the astonishment of Martha, or the joy of Gretchen? I will not attempt to describe it.

"Now that you are a hero, Harry," Gretchen said, "there is no reason why you should ever leave me again." She was weeping tears of joy.

I leave it to be imagined if the return of Professor Hardwigg created a sensation in Hamburg. Thanks to the indiscretion of Martha, the news of his departure for the interior of the earth had been spread over the whole world.

No one would believe it — and when they saw him safely back they believed it even less.

But the presence of Hans and many stray scraps of information modified public opinion by degrees.

My uncle became a great man and I, the nephew of a great man — which is something. Hamburg gave a festival in our honor. A public meeting of the Johanneum Institute was held, at which the professor related the whole story of his adventures, omitting only the facts in connection with the compass.

That same day he deposited in the archives of the town the document he had found written by Saknussemm. He expressed his great regret that circumstances stronger than his will did not allow him to follow the Icelandic traveler's track into the very center of the earth. He was modest in his glory, but his reputation only increased.

So much honor created many envious enemies for him. As his theories, supported by certain facts, contradicted the system of science based on the existence of central heat, he maintained his own views both with pen and speech against the learned of every country. Although I still believe in the theory of central heat, I confess that certain circumstances, hitherto very ill defined, may modify the laws of such natural phenomena.

At the moment when these questions were being discussed with interest, my uncle received a rude shock — one that he felt very much. Hans, despite everything my uncle could say to the contrary, left Hamburg. The man to whom we owed so much would not allow us to pay our deep debt of gratitude. He was taken with nostalgia, a love for his Icelandic home.

"Farvel," said he, one day. And with this one short word of adieu, he started for Reykjavik, which he soon reached in safety.

We were deeply attached to our brave

guide. He will never be forgotten by those lives he saved, and I hope, at some not too distant day, to see him again.

To conclude, I may say that our journey into the interior of the earth created an enormous sensation throughout the civilized world. It was translated and printed in many languages. All the leading journals published extracts from it, which were discussed, attacked, and supported with equal vigor by those who believed in it, and by those who were utterly incredulous.

Wonderful! During his lifetime my uncle enjoyed all the glory he deserved. He was even offered a large sum of money by Mr. Barnum to exhibit himself in the United States. And I am informed by a traveler that he is to be seen in wax at Madame Tussaud's!

But one care preyed upon his mind, a care which rendered him very unhappy. One fact remained inexplicable — the behavior of the compass. For a learned man to be baffled by such an inexplicable phenomenon was very aggravating. But heaven was merciful, and in the end my uncle was happy.

One day, while he was putting some minerals belonging to his collection in order, I came upon the famous compass and examined it keenly.

For six months it had lain unnoticed and untouched.

I looked at it with curiosity, which soon became surprise. I gave a loud cry. The professor, who was nearby, soon joined me.

"What is the matter?" he cried.

"The compass!"

"What about it?"

"Why its needle points to the south and not to the north."

"My dear boy, you must be dreaming."

"I am not dreaming. See, the poles are changed."

"Changed!"

My uncle put on his spectacles, examined the instrument, and leaped for joy, shaking the whole house.

A light flashed in our minds.

"I have it!" he cried, as soon as he had recovered the use of his speech. "After we arrived at Cape Saknussemm the needle of this compass pointed to the south instead of the north. But to what phenomenon do we owe this alteration in the needle?"

"Very simple."

"Explain yourself, my boy."

"During the storm on the Central Sea, the ball of fire which made a magnet of the iron in our raft, turned our compass topsy-turvy."

"Ah!" cried the professor, with a loud and ringing laugh. "It was a trick of electricity."

From that hour my uncle was the happiest of learned men, and I the happiest of ordinary mortals. As for my pretty girl, she took her place in the house in the Konigstrasse in the double role of niece and wife.

We need scarcely mention that her uncle was the illustrious Professor Hardwigg, corresponding member of all the scientific, geographical, mineralogical, and geological societies of the world.